This book is a work of fiction. The characters are a result of the author's imagination. The places are real but they have been edited and adapted to the story.

Any analogy with facts, places and people, alive or deceased, is purely coincidental.

Copyright 2022 © Stefania Cappelli – A corner on the terrace.

All rights reserved to the author.

Any abuse deriving from plagiarizing, counterfeiting, copying, distributing, marketing and publishing the material, and financial or advertising exploitation of its contents will be prosecuted under civil and criminal law as it represents a violation of copyright law (L.633/41).

ISBN: 9798354927111

Editing by Giada Obelisco.

Proofreading and translation by Simona Ubertiello.

Graphics and layout by Domenica Lupia.

Cover image by Andrea Ucini

Author's contacts: Facebook: Stefania Cappelli
Instagram: cappelli_stefania

STEFANIA CAPPELLI

A CORNER ON THE TERRACE

Part One

1

Spring was finally beginning. During the day the temperatures were gradually increasing without upsetting too much those who, like me, suffer when degrees centigrade are marked in red. I was happy, a little sun was needed. I had left the city still immersed in a dense, cold and rainy winter, and I was happy to find it in an explosion of colors. Green fields and blooming hedges framed my car journey and it filled me with joy even if, I don't deny it, it sometimes distracted me from paying attention to the road. There are two things that distract me when I'm behind the wheel: the landscape and the rearview mirror that I always keep pointed at me. Not out of vanity, but out of company, so when a song is worth singing out loud to on the radio I don't feel alone doing it. The person in the mirror and I are good at keeping each other company.

I was just starting a duet to OneRepublic's *Counting Stars* when the ringer of my phone rang in the cockpit.

"Hi! I'm parking in the front yard, where are you?" I said answering the call.

"Great. I'm in the studio, I'll be back late, see you tomorrow for breakfast. Welcome back."

The discussion we had had prior to my trip had been pending ever since, and I wasn't quite sure what to expect from our next meeting.

I entered the house and, after taking off my shoes that I left at the entrance with the luggage, I crossed the hallway to arrange the work equipment in the study. I opened the window and the light burst into the room, illuminating the layer of dust that had formed on the desk top. I put my camera down on there, as tired as I was from the effort. During the whole trip back I had dreamed of the hot bath that I would take as soon as I arrived. I turned on the tap, arranging the mixers so that the temperature was ideal and, waiting for the tub to fill with water and soft white foam, I walked around the house. That way, empty and silent, it seemed even bigger.

Passing from room to room I stopped to take a general look and at the same time readjust to my surroundings. The floorboards creaked where I expected them to, I noticed the pleasant contact of bare feet on the natural wood we had wanted in each room.

The kitchen was neat and clean, the large rectangular table seemed bare without the vase of fresh flowers that I usually liked to place in the center. The cushions in our room were stacked on the teal green velvet chair and, without them, the bed looked like the station that the military in the barracks lay out every morning, impeccably stiff. There were no open books on the coffee table in the living room, no blankets resting on the yellow armchair in front of the fireplace, let alone the smell of burnt wood in the air, although the evening temperatures still allowed us to warm up in front of the fire.

A silent neatness reigned supreme without leaving room for any signs of life within those walls. Like when you leave your "lived-in" hotel room in the morning and return in the evening to find it impeccable, as if you were entering it for the first time.

I went to enjoy the hot bath thinking about which flowers to buy the next day to put on the kitchen table.

Daisies.

The following morning Lorenzo and I were a couple sitting at the table having breakfast again, a cup of coffee in one hand and a newspaper in the other, before starting our respective days of work.

"Did you sleep well?" was his opening question.

"So good I didn't even hear you get into bed, did you come back late?"

"It was eleven thirty, but I didn't want to wake you up. How was your trip?"

"Not very good. The camera fell on the second day, I took crooked photos for two days before I could fix the problem. I expect it will take me a long time to repair the damage before handing everything over to the boss."

I imagined already sitting at the computer with my eyes tired from the many hours spent in front of the screen. It was the part of my job that I liked the least: if I could have adjusted the photos by hand, printing them on a painter's canvas, I would have preferred it.

"For real? Did you tell me about it? I do not

remember."

"Mhmm… I don't remember either. Maybe not."

"I'm sorry anyway," replied Lorenzo, getting back to reading the newspaper.

"How did you go manage without me for almost a month?" I asked, forcing him to look away from the news of the day once more.

"Nothing in particular, I took the opportunity of working more."

As if it were possible.

I knew Lorenzo would be a career man ever since we met on numerous bus trips when I was still in high school, and he was in college. He had a dedication to studying and a hunger for success that left little doubt about how his career as a grown man would go. I found this characteristic extremely attractive at the time, because it gave me a sense of responsibility that made me feel safe.

I was eighteen and sitting on the bus on my way back from school when he asked to sit next to me. I had immediately found him attractive but shyness had prevented me from talking to him, leaving that journey silent and, at least for me, slightly embarrassing. But the extraordinary amount of times the seat next to mine was the only one free each time Lorenzo got on the bus had given us the opportunity to introduce ourselves, talk, and then get to know each other well enough to find each other interesting. We had started dating, beyond the bus, when one day Lorenzo showed up at the school exit and offered me a ride in his car.

"It's very cold today, will you allow me to take you home?" he had told me, with an eagerness that I had found irresistible. I was not used to such shrewdness on the part of boys my age who, while funny and often attractive, were not very inclined to the romantic gallantry that I loved. In short, I wanted to be courted and I had been, elegantly, by Lorenzo.

During that journey we talked about the future and what we would like to do as grown ups.

"Are you going to enroll in economics next year? My faculty is also in that area." His tone betrayed a slight embarrassment that I had found very sweet.

"Actually, I don't think I'll continue my economics studies. It's not the right path for me. I would like to study photography." Lorenzo seemed surprised by my answer, perhaps even upset. After all, unlike me, he was already on the path he had chosen to reach his goal and was working hard to soon become an established doctor.

It was only after graduation that he decided to specialize in cosmetic surgery. The enthusiasm with which he projected himself into the role of a *doctor* wearing a white coat and a gold plate on the door of the study was overwhelming.

At the time I had no idea how much loneliness this dedication to work would bring into my life, but after all my work leads me to travel often, and I certainly could not define myself as a *housewife*.

Lorenzo got up from the table to clear his breakfast, asked me if I wanted more coffee and, when I answered affirmatively, filled my cup.

"I have to go, are you going out or are you staying home?"

"I'll be here to work on the photos."

"Okay, well, see you tonight, have a nice day."

" You too."

Neither of us had touched on the subject of our last

fight, but I didn't even expect one of us to. It was not an early morning conversation.

Lorenzo walked out of the kitchen, shortly after I heard the front door close and I was alone again.

I sat at the table for a few moments with a cup of hot coffee in my hands in the comfort of a house which, despite everything, I had missed a lot. Eventually I got up and went to take off my pajamas and put on comfortable clothes that made me feel more active. Although I often worked from home, I couldn't focus while wearing a nightgown. A few minutes later I was sitting at my desk, ready for the long work of reviewing the material.

I spent the whole morning in front of the screen arranging the trip photos. Myanmar had given me landscapes that still sent me back to a state of profound inner stillness. I had already walked on those lands several years before, when the journey had no other purpose than that of life experience. In those ten years the country had profoundly changed and looking for new places, little or not at all beaten by mass tourism, had not been as easy as it was back then.

When I first went there, Inle Lake and its still waters - on which the Intha fishermen paddle around with just their leg work, standing on the unstable wooden boats - were still something incredible, unexplored.

Despite the advent of tourism, however, I must admit that the stretch of red pagodas in Bagan, which at sunset light up like flames resting on an intense green lawn under a partly still blue sky, had had the same effect of wonder in me as the first time.

At twenty-two I had taken that trip differently, no comfortable beds or clean bathrooms, I traveled on local buses and ate a little here and there, and what I could find. My guide at the time was called Kukumar:

a fantastic Burmese woman who knew every corner of that wonderful land and talked about it honestly, without hiding her worries about a future that seemed to be running too fast towards modernization. And it was her again, Kukumar, ten years later, who guided me to the enchanting places of that country that she still called Burma, always traveling on local vehicles but sleeping on slightly more comfortable beds and... with a private bathroom.

Going through one photograph after another, I found myself in front of the most significant faces I had come across during the trip. Luminous smiles, eyes that, like quicksand, swallow you up to let you enter the soul of whoever is watching you. As always, in the end, it is people who make a trip.

The image of the two Buddhist monks, in the respectful silence that accompanies the parade to get the only meal of the day, brought me back to the northern areas, where tourism was not yet an intrusive presence and a Western woman was almost an attraction for both adults and children. I watched those two wonderful boys on the screen, with a clean and smooth face and a rigor in their posture that left no room for frivolity of any kind, which in our world is the norm for their peers.

I thought back to Lorenzo's question: "How was the trip?" and I wondered why I had answered that way, zeroing in on the story about my camera which, after all, had been the only negative of that month.

Who knows why I decided to deliver that boring detail, when in reality I could have nailed him to the chair for hours telling him about the wonders of that country and how much I had liked it. Again.

Without being able to find an answer, I noticed that it was almost lunchtime and my eyes needed a break.

It was the right time to go buy flowers.

Getting into the car, I called Lisa, inviting her for a quick lunch. I had missed talking to her lately.

"Wow, great idea! So you can tell me about the trip. At one o'clock at our usual spot", was her enthusiastic reply.

Lisa and I had chosen each other as best friends on the second day of first grade, sharing desks and, later on, practically our entire lives. There was no lack of laughter together, but also tears, secrets and insanity. Each of my more or less significant steps were supported by the realization of always finding support in her. We grew up together while attending different schools, different universities, distant paths from each other. However, nothing has ever changed between her and I, our relationship has grown with us becoming a friendship for which I feel deeply grateful.

Arriving at the bar after stopping by the florist, I sat down at the table and placed a bouquet of pink peonies on it. I knew Lisa would like them.

We usually competed to see who could be even more late but, despite my attempts to beat her, she had won again this time. Once she had forgotten the appointment completely and had left me sitting at the bar for more than an hour waiting in vain for her. Since that day I have always tried to put very little distance between the planning of the meeting and the meeting itself.

While waiting, I picked up the book that I had started reading on the plane and that I kept in my bag in case the opportunity arose to carry on with a few chapters. I turned it over in my hands but then placed it on the table and looked around. The place was crowded and the humming of people chatting in the background filled the space around me. The room was very bright thanks to a glass window as large as the entire wall. The light broke in on the wooden tables and, passing through the colored glasses lined up on the counter, created enchanting plays of light. A kaleidoscope of colors.

Lisa arrived visibly out of breath, but with her usual poise. She was wearing a burgundy-colored jacket and pantsuit, a white blouse with neck embroidery, and her dark hair, albeit wavy, was neatly trimmed in a bob that barely covered her ears.

"Here I am, sorry, there was traffic, I was stuck at work, my son spilled juice on my pants, I broke a heel. Choose the excuse you like best, you know I'm late because I can't deal."

How could I not love her?

The waiter instantly appeared in front of us. I had already caught him a couple of times, watching me from a distance while I waited. In the rush hour of lunch, keeping a table busy for a long time without consuming anything was frowned upon by the dining room staff.

"Good morning ladies, would you like to order?" the young man asked politely, already armed with a pen and paper.

"Yes, we would, but only if you promise me you'll never call us ladies again." The young man's clean shaven face lit up like an induction cooker at Lisa's words, who promptly distracted him from his embarrassment. "I was kidding, dear, I'd like your emmer salad, if you have it, and sparkling water, please."

I ordered the same thing, but replaced the sparkling water with still water, forcing myself to hold back a laugh.

"You just can't bite your tongue, can you?"

"Why would I? He is young and it is only right for him to learn. Besides, at thirty-two, I'm still not ready to be called a *lady* for the rest of my life." She buried her face in the bouquet to breathe in its scent. "Peonies, how wonderful."

"I knew you would appreciate them. How are you?" I asked, biting into a piece of bread, taken from the basket that the unlucky waiter had brought to the table.

"The usual, I'm working a lot but things are really good at the firm. You know, Pietro's first tooth fell out yesterday."

"How sweet, his first tooth. Wow, it seems like just yesterday you told me it was coming out. "

"I know, I was thinking the same thing."

The arrival of Lisa's child had been a significant event, I know it is for everyone, but Lisa and Carlo had struggled for years before they could conceive. Their decision to have a child immediately after marriage was due to the fact that Lisa feared that, once she became a lawyer, she would not be able to dedicate the necessary time and attention to motherhood. Thus, they found themselves, very young, already faced with a reality which was difficult to accept, and which had also put their marriage to a severe test. But then, over time, they were able to accept the idea of being just the two of them, learning to be enough for one another. I remember being struck by the extraordinary strength with which their love had faced that suffering. Sometime later, by that time unexpectedly, Pietro got here. Perhaps that soul, destined for the two of them, had just wanted to give them time to strengthen the foundation of their relationship before arriving, aware of the earthquake it would cause.

"Look, I brought you some photos, I just printed them." I handed them to her and told her about Myanmar as if I were still there. I tried to convey the same emotions I had felt walking around those places and meeting the people whose faces she was admiring. Lisa seemed enraptured by my words and listened to me like a child during a bedtime story. At the end of my tale she told me: "You should also write the articles about the trips you take, you are good at taking pictures, but when you tell stories you are hypnotic."

I thought back to the answer about the trip I had given Lorenzo that morning, and I told her about it.

"I have a theory on it, but I don't know if you want to hear it," she said, looking at me seriously. Quite astonished, I asked her to go on and she pressed on with a direct question: "Is your work as important as Lorenzo's?"

I was dumbfounded, I had no idea what she meant. "My work is important to me."

"I mean..." she resumed without considering my answer, "your mother never failed to let you know how much she didn't think photography was a real job. And your father never took a stand on it, out of fear of rocking the boat. But I remember well, how it hurt you not to have their support. Should we talk about your in-laws? Or, better yet... your mother-in-law, who keeps telling you that you don't have time to give her a grandchild, because you travel the world playing with your camera?"

"What you said is all true, but I don't understand what this has to do with Lorenzo, he never had anything to say about my work."

"Lorenzo has never opposed your path, but he has never supported it. He has simply never given much importance to what you do for a living, because he is the breadwinner, he brings the money into the house and huge amounts of it, too. You could have been a photographer, a baker, or a crocheter, Lorenzo would have never really cared." She stopped to drink a glass of water and went on: "I think you gave him that answer because you needed to make him understand that yours is a real job and that it is not always easy. You don't need to do the same with me, because you know that I admire what you do, so you feel free to tell me how much you loved that trip, without fearing I would think you had taken a vacation."

I gasped, my gaze fixed on her lips looking for a signal that would let me know she was joking. Okay, we had lived the episodes with my parents together, since I always told her every argument that my choice generated within the walls of our home, but this? I had never told her I felt subordinate to my husband. It was her idea and I can't deny that it annoyed me to hear her express it in that way.

Lisa stared at my troubled expression and said, "I know you don't like what I'm saying, but I don't want to be hypocritical to you, Anna. We have never been with one another. I don't want you to agree with me, but please think about it."

"Maybe you should have been a therapist, not a lawyer," I said with a hint of a smile in an attempt to bring some light-heartedness back into the conversation.

"I pay my therapist top dollar every Monday morning, that's why I'm so knowledgeable," she replied, accepting my change of direction.

A spontaneous laugh brightened up the moment,

allowing us to return to our ember salad and finish our lunch by chatting about less demanding topics.

I had not yet told Lisa about the argument I had with Lorenzo before my trip. I admit that I was going to do it but, after hearing her words, I didn't feel like it anymore. After all, I hadn't been able to process it myself yet, and I don't imagine I would have enjoyed her bluntness. I had the impression that she was more clear-headed than I about my relationship with Lorenzo.

2

Back home that afternoon I went back to the computer in an attempt to finish the task, which I should have handed in by the end of the week, as soon as possible. I spent the following days without too many distractions, helped by a gray and rainy March that did not seem ready to leave Winter yet.

On Friday morning I was ready to deliver the material and I got up excited to leave the house and return to social life.

"Excellent as always, Anna," said Angelo, the editor in chief, after examining the photos I had brought him. Then, looking away from the images, he added: "You're free."

He caught me off guard. "What do you mean?"

"You are free for the next few months. I have no trips planned for you until October."

"Wow, until October?"

"You have traveled a lot in the last year, we have people who can replace you for the next articles. You can take some time. "

In fact, in the previous twelve months I had been abroad at intervals of about two months for periods of approximately three to four weeks per trip.

"And where are you sending me in October?" I asked to set a date on the calendar.

"I don't know, we have all Summer ahead of us," he replied smiling, as if he recognized in my question the frenzy of knowing what the next destination would be. Actually my concern was more about the amount of time I would be unemployed.

Him dismissing me for such a long time had never happened before, perhaps it was not enough to fear for my job position, but that decision on his part gave me an uneasy, alarming feeling.

Realizing that I would not have received other information, I replied with a simple "Okay" adding that, in any case, I would not have occupied my down time differently, making myself available for last minute assignments.

Leaving the newsroom I carried that unpleasant feeling with me, trying not to let it weigh me down too much. Certainly, as he had said, all in all I deserved some rest.

I had been working as a photographer for ten years. For five, my efforts had benefited Angelo's online travel magazine. We mainly dealt with countries not yet invaded by mass tourism. I was given the luxury of being taken to spectacular locations before they were marred by the massive construction of hotels and restaurants.

Other collaborators, on the other hand, took care of writing the articles.

I have always found it absurd that whoever wrote the articles did not visit the places they were reporting about beforehand, but when I had volunteered for that role, Angelo had nipped all my expectations in the bud.

"You take phenomenal photographs and that's what I want from you." Since that time, in fact, I hadn't felt like asking him again.

After dinner that evening, I couldn't get what Angelo said out of my head, I caught myself several times staring into space, standing in front of the sink, rinsing the dishes before putting them in the dishwasher. Lorenzo was still sitting at the table and my mind started wandering creating some of the most catastrophic and, I admit, quite unlikely scenarios. I pictured myself knocking on the door of all the editorial offices in Northern Italy trying to convince them of what I was capable of in my work. And it terrified me. Especially since I had never had to do a proper interview. At the beginning of my career I was selling travel photos on my personal website which I kept updated daily. It was lovely but unprofitable. I had begun to realize that I needed a more profitable job when Angelo contacted me, right on my page, telling me that he was fascinated by my photographs and that he wanted me in his staff at all costs. Enticed by his offer, I found myself working for him within a couple of weeks.

We had agreed on a minimum number of trips per year which, to sum it up, would have guaranteed me a more stable and undoubtedly higher income than the previous one.

But the company was thriving back then: it was one of the first to throw itself into communication exclusively via the Web and the market's response had been excellent from the beginning. In a very short time they had gone from a tiny newsroom in an attic owned by Angelo - then the sole owner of the company - to a gigantic open space on the seventeenth floor on Piazza Gae Aulenti.

I had already arrived in the second location and I remember immediately loving the choice of a shared workspace, no separate offices, no assigned workstations, only work areas marked by large wooden tables, some round, others rectangular, which brought harmony to the environment making it friendly and warm.

Even in this, the company had been an innovator.

"Does that plate seem clean enough to just me, or are you trying to pierce the porcelain?" Lorenzo asked bringing me back to reality. I was so engrossed that I didn't hear him approach or observe me.

"I'm worried," I told him quickly.

"About what?"

"Today Angelo told me something strange and I'm not happy about it."

"What did he tell you that upset you so much?"

I told him about the conversation Angelo and I had had in the afternoon and, at the end of my story, he remained motionless, as if he found nothing disturbing in what he had heard.

"I don't understand your concern," he said in a tone that sounded almost annoyed.

"I'm worried this period of suspension will anticipate something worse," I continued, seeing him still dumbfounded. "There are other people who are making their way into the editorial team, young people who the company can pay much less than what it pays me and who allow it to benefit from preferential tax relief."

"But they don't have any experience!"

"They are people who have a school education and, even if they have no practice in the field yet, they will. I'm not saying that I'm afraid of being fired tomorrow, but that the company is making room young people to bring them to the level of someone who has my experience, to then take our place."

Lorenzo looked at me as if I were saying I believed in Santa Claus.

"There are people who can replace me on future trips," I emphasized Angelo's words, with the look of someone who is explaining a basic concept to a four-year-old child.

"What are you saying, Anna, come on! You're the most coveted photographer in there. Plus you know that Angelo has a soft spot for you. He would gladly see you after work, if it were up to him!"

Not only was he not giving any importance to my concern, but he was actually shifting the focus to my boss's complacent attitude. As if up until that moment I had been successful at my job because of it.

"I am good but I am also one of the highest paid. If they needed to make cuts, I'd be someone to consider!"

"How come you are not denying it? You usually get angry when I drop hints about Angelo wooing you."

"I didn't even notice. I'm worried and you're not listening to me", I lied.

I definitely had noticed, but I didn't want to change the subject so I continued: "They have been hiring young interns for months and last winter Michael made two trips to China and one to Papua New Guinea. Those are usually my territories, you know?"

"Anna, please, don't get anxious about nothing as you always do. They don't want to fire you", he said, placing his plate in the sink. "And, even if they were, we don't need your salary, we can live very well on what I earn, you know."

There they were, the worst words he could say.

Lisa's speech during lunch a few days ago had remained a silent presence in my memory and now my mind had turned up the volume on her words. *"He never paid any attention to what you do because he is the breadwinner."*

It terrified me that she might be right and I had naïvely never realized it.

Of course I knew, he earned enough to support a family with five children, and we didn't even have one. That wasn't the point: even though I had always cared about my financial independence, it wasn't money that made my hands sweaty at the thought of losing my job. It was what the journey represented for me, how I felt when I was away, how I always, unfailingly, rediscovered the woman I knew I was but couldn't express in my everyday life.

"I'm not talking about money. I don't want to lose my job. It's my life." I uttered that, while I resumed filling the dishwasher, turning my back on him. Even though I didn't see his expression, I knew him enough to know he didn't like those words.

"You're not losing your job. Stop that." He had decided that the matter was closed. He left, leaving me alone in the kitchen.

From a distance I heard the ringtone of my phone. I assumed he was buried in my work bag and that meant not being able to answer in time. In fact, I got to it when it had already stopped ringing.

Missed call: Mom

If I had called her back she would have understood that something was wrong with my tone for some magical power that mothers have, in any case I had no desire to explain. I turned the phone off and went to sleep.

3

Opening my eyes, still wrapped under my warm blanket, the thoughts of work and the argument with Lorenzo of a few evenings before invaded my mind. That morning, however, I shook them off and, realizing I had to get out of the lethargic state in which I was slipping, I decided to get dressed and search for a piece of paradise.

Not far from home there was a sumptuous historic building which housed the large municipal library. Inside there was a large room with shelves full of volumes that reached the very high ceilings. It reminded me of the library the Beast gave Belle in the Disney cartoon. The lamps on the wooden tables gave off a warm light suitable for reading, making the environment as welcoming as a domestic living room. Often the silence in the air was so profound that one could only hear the pages turning.

Outside, the white of the facade contrasted with the bright green of the lawns and the foliage of the trees that surrounded it. The pond with its still waters completed that image of perfection.

I loved spending my time in that place, immersing myself in my favorite novels and sitting in the shade of its oak on sunny days. When it was time to get up and go home, I closed the book and stayed a few minutes more to observe the people who filled the park.

There were always mothers who encouraged their little ones to interact with the ducks in the pond, I found them very sweet. I liked to imagine what they had been like before they entered the whirlwind of motherhood. Some I pictured as career women in high heels and suits, busy giving lectures hypnotizing their audience. A bit like Lisa. I imagined others as less ambitious, with a more easygoing lifestyle, with the desire to create a welcoming home that smelled of vanilla biscuits.

In any case, I found them beautiful.

Then, in late afternoon, young couples occupied the park benches until the sun went down; without saying much, they spent hours kissing. They too were stunning, with so much life ahead of them, unaware of how much those long and silent kisses, over time, would give way to words.

That day, in search of my little corner of paradise, I decided to go there, looking for new books and motivation.

I was sitting under the big tree without being able to pay attention to the book's pages. My thoughts had remained anchored to Angelo's speech and I understood that I had to get explanations in order to free my mind. I took out the phone from my bag and dialed his number.

I was also willing to confess my concern to him if I didn't get satisfactory answers.

"Hi Anna," answered a female voice, it was Angelo's secretary.

"Hi Giorgia, how are you?" I asked her unprepared to hear her voice.

"All right, Angelo is in the conference room with the partners."

"Damn, serious stuff?" I asked jokingly, even though I was looking for information.

"I'm starting to wonder too, they've been locked in there for hours." She spoke in such a low voice that I imagined her hand in front of her mouth whispering in secret. Then, raising her tone again, she added, "Do you want to leave a message for him?"

I had a horrible feeling that my omen was taking shape.

"Just tell him I called, thanks."

"Will do, have a good day."

"Right back at you."

I had not learned anything new with that call, yet it seemed to me I had an extra element to worry about.

I knew that Angelo would never want to fire me, but wasn't certain about the rest of the management team. Indeed, the fact that the other members did not actively participate in the life of the editorial staff gave me the idea that for them we were numbers rather than people.

I gathered my things and tried to clear my mind by taking a walk in the park. The bright green of the lawn was like an injection of calm into my stormy soul. The foliage of the trees contrasted with the clear blue of the sky, the song of the birds revived a timid spring, the sun illuminated the pink of the cherry trees in bloom and the air was fresh and fragrant. A coat was still needed when walking, but you could feel the changing of seasons. I thought that, shortly thereafter, even the clothing would be lighter.

I stopped in my tracks, hearing the phone ring, took it out of my coat pocket and saw Lisa's name on the display.

"Good morning," I replied in a shrill voice.

"Hi, sorry if I'm bothering you but I need a favor." Her tone, on the other hand, was worried, so I realized that something had happened.

"What happened?"

"The school called me, it seems that Pietro got hurt playing football, they said it's nothing serious but his nose is bleeding and they want me to go and get him." She paused to take a breath and continued in an anguished voice: "I'm in court and I can't leave now, Carlo is not answering his phone and I was wondering, if you're around, if you can drop by and get him."

"Of course, I'm on my way," I assured her.

"Please call me as soon as you see him and tell me how he is. I feel awful for not being able to go to him."

"Don't worry, I'll call you shortly."

"Okay, I'll be waiting. Anna ... Thank you so much."

In her voice, I could hear a mother's frustration fighting the demands of her career. It was a condition Lisa had often told me about, and I understood the guilt that was gripping her.

I arrived at Pietro's school in a few minutes, parked the car in the place reserved for teachers so as not to waste time and walked quickly to the secretariat.

Although Lisa had already told me that it was nothing more than a bloody nose, I felt some anxiety in anticipation of seeing him and I waited for the return of the secretary who had gone to pick him up from her class, rubbing my hands nervously.

"Holy crap!" I exclaimed when I saw him walking towards me through the hall of the school. He had a swollen forehead, a color that faded from purple to green, and two white tips protruding from his nostrils. "Darling, how are you?"

"Fine, fine, don't worry, auntie. Are you seeing this? I look like an Avatar character."

I burst out laughing. Pietro has always called me auntie ever since he was a little thing, just ninety centimeters tall. Even though we have no blood ties, it is understandable that he has always considered me and her mother as sisters.

"You're crazy! What happened?" I asked, relieved to hear him so lively.

"I saved a penalty... with my face," he replied, proud of his prowess.

I was about to ask if they were playing medicine ball football when my phone rang.

"It's your mom, you answer so you can calm her down." I handed him the phone.

"Hey, ma, what is it?" Hearing him speak like that filled me with tenderness, he didn't seem worried in the least, much less had it frightened him to get a blow like that between the eyes. He seemed amused by the weirdness of that day, without suspecting the anguish that the event had generated around him. While he was still on the phone with Lisa bombarding him with questions, I heard him answer, "No, it was a basketball." I guessed Lisa had asked him the same question I was going to ask him. Peter's answer justified the bruised face.

"She wants to talk to you," he said at one point, handing the phone back to me.

"Hey, Lisa."

"Listen, how does it look? Do you think he needs a doctor?"

"He is in great shape, it doesn't like his nose is bleeding anymore but he has a nice bruise on his forehead. I think ice is enough but if it's going to make you feel better, I will take him to the pediatrician."

"I talked to Carlo, he's in Como, I forgot he was going to be there today. I still have a couple more hours here, if it's not necessary for me to come to him right away."

"No urgency whatsoever. Really, I'll stay with Pietro until your arrival."

"Okay, thank you very much. Maybe, if you don't mind taking a trip to the pediatrician, it would reassure me."

"I'll take him right away, see you later... and stay calm."

In the car on our way to the clinic, Pietro looked curiously out of the window, I guessed he wanted to observe what happens in the city when he is usually at school. It reminded me of a day when I was a child and my father took me for blood tests. After picking me up, we went to the bar in the square for breakfast and he ordered a latte for me, with cocoa on top and a cream donut.

"If mom knew, she'd kill me," he said, handing me the saucer, and I laughed proudly at our complicity. All morning I had accompanied him on the stops he had to make for work. I remember the feeling of euphoria I felt in being able to be with him during the hours when it was never possible for me to do so. Seeing what he did while I was usually in school, meeting the people he talked about with mom in the evening when he told her about his day. I had the opportunity to observe that man in the moments when he was not just my dad. I followed him when he visited his customers, he was always smiling, some offered him coffee, he told jokes with others, he inquired about the health of their wives and children, and only at the end did they talk about work. People seemed to trust him a lot. Before we went out, each of them would give me a candy or a treat. I had thought then that his life was really beautiful.

When we got to the pediatrician, we sat in the waiting room. My inexperience in things like this had made me overlook the detail that there could be many other mothers waiting in line. I admit that there and then I considered postponing the visit but looking at Peter's forehead, at least an inch thicker, I gave up.

"Do you want me to read you a book?" I suggested to pass the time. At the back of the room was a nice bookcase with a sign saying *"leave your used book here"*. This way, many children could donate the texts they would have abandoned as they grew up, for the benefit of the little ones who were about to be initiated into the fantastic world of fairy tales.

"Yes, I'm going to choose it", he replied.

As Pietro was walking away, a mother sitting next to me approached me as if she wanted to share a secret. "Was he beaten?" he asked, pointing to Pietro.

I turned to look at her with wide eyes, horrified by that question. "No", I replied dryly.

"Uh... So what happened to him?"

"I don't think it's any of your business, but if you're so curious why don't you ask him yourself?" I answered in an attempt to silence her.

Meanwhile, Peter was hopping back with a book

in hand.

I looked at the colorful cover and the title made me smile *"Everything is hard before it gets easy"*. I thought that Peter was already wiser than me.

I started reading the book when the lady's voice interrupted us: "What happened to your forehead, little one?"

Really?

"I saved a penalty... with my face" Pietro replied, still proud of what had happened, then, without waiting for the next question, he added: "It was a basketball."

"And why did you play soccer with a basketball?" the suspicious lady insisted.

"Because the one we use for football was over the net, in the parish courtyard."

The interrogation was cut short by the arrival of the pediatrician ready to call in a new little patient.

"Well, well, well, who do we have here? Pietro, what a beautiful face you have! Tell the truth... you got tired of being in school today!" the doctor said seeing us in the room without an appointment. Pietro smiled at him and went over to the doctor who held out his hand. "Let's go," said the doctor, "I'll see you right away, a rock like you didn't even feel anything, I bet."

I gathered our jackets and followed them into the room.

"Nothing serious, mommy! An ointment to put on the bruise and your boy will be as good as new in a couple of days!" I told Lisa once I left the office.

After spending some time in the park playing, we got hungry and we went to lunch, when Pietro took off his jacket I saw that the sweatshirt was stained with blood and, smiling, I suggested that we go shopping to buy a new one. I figured Lisa would feel bad seeing her son come home in bloody clothes.

After a trip to the mall, two Avengers T-shirts in the bag and a proudly worn Jurassic World sweatshirt, it was time to go home.

Lisa was waiting for us in the kitchen and welcomed Pietro with a big hug, he proudly showed her the ball scratches and, after showing her our purchases, he zoomed to his room to play.

"Where does that child find the energy? All day long he runs, jumps, laughs, talks and never stops. He never seems to need a break to recharge."

"They are like that, they recharge at night and while they eat. That's enough to keep them active for a whole day."

"It is a pity we lose that ability when we become adults."

"In part it is lost with age and in part we give it up."

"What do you mean?"

"Well... do you have the same energy when you travel as you do when you stay home?"

"Actually, no."

"That's the point, when you travel and you love what you do your batteries naturally recharge... like a dynamo. The more you ride, the more you generate energy. Eventually you are physically tired but inside you are still active. Children are like that, and even some adults who have understood the trick."

I nodded to Lisa's words, she seemed to be getting wiser as the years went by. I didn't know if she was among those adults who discovered the trick, or if she was simply hyperactive. She certainly had a lot of willpower to be able to be a loving mother and have such a demanding job. But she seemed happy despite the effort.

I went to the window, the sky was taking on shades of red and I realized that I hadn't heard from Lorenzo all day. Maybe I should have called him or at least let him know where I was.

"Do you want to stay for dinner? It will only be the three of us because Carlo will be back late."

Actually, I didn't have too much desire to go home to face a silent dinner with Lorenzo, talkativeness was not our characteristic and, considering that we were also fresh from having an argument, I could imagine the negative aura that would have hovered over our heads.

"Gladly," I replied, "I'll tell Lorenzo and then help you set the table."

I called his cell phone, but the answering machine answered.

I left a message telling him that I was staying with Lisa and that I would be back after dinner.

We ate in the kitchen on an informally laid table: placemats instead of tablecloths, glasses all different from each other, paper napkins. A table that I found cheerful and simple.

Lisa told me that she would probably have to take a trip to Barcelona for a few days and she didn't feel like it. At the end of dinner she took Pietro to bed, at last he seemed to cave.

I began clearing the table and when Lisa returned I had already started the dishwasher.

"Oh, thank you," she said with the narrow eyes of someone returning to the light after being in the dark for a while.

"Don't even think about it. Did he fall asleep? "

"Collapsed as soon as the story was over."

I was about to tell her to go and rest too, when I saw her open a bottle of Barolo. I took two glasses from the cupboard and we sat down on the sofa. Lisa lit the gas fireplace with the remote control. There was no warmth, but its glow was pleasant nonetheless.

"Look, Anna, I wanted to tell you that I've been thinking about what I told you at lunch the other day, I'm sorry, I think I was too blunt. Sometimes I go too far without weighing the effect my words may have on others. I'm sorry if I annoyed you with what I said about Lorenzo."

I looked at her for a few moments, gathering my thoughts and then, placing the glass of wine on the table, I told her about the discussion we had had a few nights before about my job and about how real her interpretation had seemed to me.

She listened to me without giving any other opinions, simply accepting my words and the frustration they were imbued with.

In the end she just said to me: "Every now and then ask yourself if you are happy, it will serve as a compass to understand if you are on the right path." She looked at me winking her right eye and then added: "A piece of advice that cost me fifty euros last Monday." We laughed together.

There was more, I had not yet told her about the fight before leaving for Myanmar and I felt the need to do it.

"There's another thing I'd like to tell you, if you're not too tired to hear me out."

"Tell me everything," she said, adjusting her position on the sofa as if she wanted to pay attention with her whole body.

"Lorenzo doesn't want children." As I said those words aloud for the first time, I felt a shiver under my skin.

Lisa looked at me with the eyes of someone who knew what it was like to have to give up thinking about motherhood.

I went on telling her about the argument, starting with dinner at Lorenzo's parents' house. She followed my words carefully, letting glances and expressions that gave away her thoughts slip here and there.

At the end of my story, when I told her that we hadn't taken up the subject since that evening, she seemed amazed. She had the expression of someone who about to tell me something I would not have liked. Again.

This time, however, she seemed more cautious, as if she were afraid to express herself, so I encouraged her by asking her to tell me what she was thinking.

With a penetrating look she asked me directly: "Do you want a child?"

I knew she was aiming straight for the heart... of the speech. "Yes, I would like one."

"Since when have you known you want one?"

I sighed realizing where she was going.

"I've always known and I know what you're thinking."

"I'm thinking I wanted a child, and I looked my husband in the face and told him straight up. Then when the child did not come and everything around us told us that we should give up, I looked my husband in the face and kept telling him I wanted a child."

"There was a time when you stopped telling him, though." I said those words in a very low voice keeping my gaze fixed on my legs, I was afraid of hurting her and offending her, but I had to go on to understand.

Lisa sighed deeply and leaned back against the sofa, her neck touching the wall and I knew what she was remembering in that instant.

"I only stopped when I had the final answer. When that door shut in my face... I stopped fighting. You want to start fighting beginning with the door in your face. That's what I don't understand." And with the kindness of someone who doesn't want to hurt you, she added: "Why didn't you tell him when it was already time for you?"

"I wondered about it during the whole trip, but without coming up with a convincing answer. I don't know why I didn't speak, I didn't fight, I didn't insist or simply because I didn't ask. Maybe change scares me deep down. Maybe I don't feel up to it."

A thousand others "maybes" were spinning in my head looking for answers and breaking certainties, but then I thought about the present moment and the fact that having a baby was no longer an option. And I suffered.

"Don't you ever feel like you're living two lives?" she asked, her dark eyes staring straight into mine.

"Why are you asking me that?"

She rolled her eyes. "I'm not telling you why, just answer me."

"Well... in a way I am. My life when I travel is very different from the one I live when I am in Milan."

"And are you different too?" I looked down, there was no need to explain why, I understood what she meant by that question. I nodded.

"And are you always happy? Whether traveling or at home?"

"Not always."

"Not always in both situations or in one, yes, and the other... not always?"

"When I travel I am happy. I know it, it has always been that way. When I arrive somewhere in the world and I am alone, I feel free. Nobody knows me and I'm not afraid to show myself for who I am, indeed, very often what in my daily reality is seen as something wrong, in the eyes of those who live in different environments it is extraordinary." I found it difficult to explain that concept. It was a feeling, something indefinable. "My job, for example, here many see it as a pastime, while in other parts of the world it is an art form. Because here a job is only a job if you kill yourself working hard to bring home the bacon, you are not allowed to turn your passion into a job. Even mothers who choose to stay at home to raise their children are seen as privileged, even ladies of leisure. When I travel I meet people who do not have the mental limits enforced by society and seem happy. Here it is, that is how I feel when I'm away, I feel like I have the opportunity to be happy, not just a day, or just a moment like when I'm here, but always. Happy all day, every day."

"And in your life here, when are you happy?"

I took a breath and looked up to find the answer somewhere in my mind. "When I'm here, I'm always happy at specific times."

"Like when?"

"Well, when you and I see each other I always am, of course." Lisa smiled and raised her glass of wine as if to toast. "And then there are other things that make me happy: reading a good book, going to the park and being in the middle of nature, sitting in front of the fireplace with a glass of wine ... but you see ... these are external things, that give me moments of lightheartedness in which I find happiness. But it's not like being happy inside, a constant state of mind."

"Have you ever wanted to move abroad? I mean ... Have you ever found yourself in a place and thought about the possibility of living there?"

I laughed. "Virtually every time."

"And would you do it?"

"Seriously, I don't think so. I would like to find a happy way to live here. To continue traveling, of course, but I'm tired of seeing my trips as an escape. I would like to feel good where I am, to feel ... full and satisfied here, as when I am away."

I looked at Lisa. She stared at me without saying a word, but what her eyes conveyed was as powerful as a truth. I lowered my gaze unable to hold hers which made me feel naked, caught in all my disguises.

For a couple of years I had noticed that change, how each trip made me feel more and more alive while coming back was just a moment of waiting, a period that I tolerated only by immersing myself in the organization of the next departure. The fact is, I was always alone. But if that loneliness on the road was the freedom to express myself, at home it felt like a prison. I worked for the editorial office but I only went there a few times, just to deliver the material and to attend meetings once a month and often those two occasions coincided. So I had colleagues, yes, but I hardly ever saw them. Lorenzo, needless to say, was locked up in his clinic from morning to evening and sometimes it was better that way. Coping with his absence when I was alone was one thing, putting up with it when we were together was really hard. I had a few friends, all married and with children who stayed home in the evening and juggled work and family commitments during the day, as did Lisa. Because of this, I thought, in the moments of happiness that I had listed I always pictured myself alone. But here I had a script, a role to portray. I was also the wife of a very respectable and esteemed doctor, and I was a daughter-in-law. In addition to having to attend family dinners, I also had to be a certain type of woman. Composed, neat, accepting. It was a life that I would not have chosen to lead if it had been offered to me ten years ago, but I believed in the possibility of changing it. I thought it was possible to find something that would bring *life* into our days.

 Lisa understood that. She didn't add anything else but, standing at the front door, before I left, she held me in a strong embrace, like a friend, or rather, a sister. I felt tears fill my eyes but, looking up at the ceiling, I tried to hold them back.

4

A month and a half earlier.

"I have to go to London on Monday, I'll be away for a few days," said Lorenzo, breaking the silence that accompanies our breakfasts. It was Friday morning and it was less than a week before my departure for Myanmar.

"When will you come back? I'm leaving on Thursday", I replied amazed by the news.

"I know you're leaving on Thursday, but I have a conference and then I'll take the opportunity to do a follow-up visit to a patient I operated on last year."

"I understand, but will we be able to see each other? How long will you be gone for?"

"I was thinking of returning on Wednesday evening."

We will shoot by each other rather than actually seeing each other.

"I could go with you. If you can stay one more day, I can leave directly from London, I have a layover there."

"I'm sorry, but I've already booked my flights and I'll be very busy, I wouldn't have time to be with you during the day."

"Ah, okay. Judging from what you told me I thought you were still planning."

I watched him get up to clear the table.

"I must have not made myself clear. What will you do today? Still preparing for the trip?" he said casually, taking my cup without asking me if I was finished.

"Yes, I have a few last errands to run then I'll go to the library." My mandatory stop before any trip.

"My parents invited us to dinner tonight, can I confirm?" he asked, drying his hands with the dish towel.

"Okay, are you going directly or will you pick me up?"

"I'll see you there," he replied, heading for the entrance to prepare to leave. Wearing the black coat that showed his poise, he reappeared at the kitchen door adding: "Anyway, we can plan a weekend in Europe, if you want."

Perhaps he had realized that he had dismissed my proposal in an unkind way and this was his way of making up for it.

"Why not?" I answered thinking that surely that would be the last time we would talk about it.

"Have a good day at work," I added as he walked away, waving to me.

Later in the afternoon, as I walked out of the library

with my book haul in my backpack, I saw that the sky had darkened quite a bit and a few drops were starting to fall. I hurried to get to the car, but the storm caught to me first. The time it took me to open the door, and I was already completely soaked. I called Lorenzo to inform him that I would be late having to go home to change. While I was talking on the phone I tried to watch the road, between a bucket of water on the windshield and the other.

"Don't go to the house, I just realized I have your set of keys. If you didn't have the bad habit of pulling the door behind you without locking it, you would have noticed it too! In any case, you can't enter, so come to my parents, you will dry off here."

I wondered how it was possible that he was the one who had made a mistake, and yet it was I who was being scolded for it.

In any case, my concern at that point was another. I didn't want to show up in that state at Lorenzo's parents' house. With them I always just happened to look a mess. My mother-in-law was a good woman, but she treated me like the "poor thing" of the family. I was the one who had a job she didn't understand, the one who wanted to get married in a park instead of having a respectful church ceremony, the one who - above all - hadn't yet given her a grandchild.

She was convinced that it was I who was refusing motherhood because I didn't want to give up my job and, of course, her son must have suffered a lot because of it.

All in all, however, I had a good relationship with Maria and I had always brushed those things off for the benefit of a quiet life.

I parked the car in my in-laws front yard and I waited a moment in the useless hope that the rain would give a moment of respite, then I ran out and took shelter under the porch.

"Anna, what have you done? Didn't you have an umbrella? Didn't you know there was rain on the forecast for tonight?" Maria greeted me at the door.

I never have an umbrella and I never look at the weather forecast, except in summer when I'm terrified that the temperatures will be too high to bear. Or while I'm traveling.

"I was in the park, it caught me off guard", I replied sadly.

"Come inside, take a shower and I'll go get you a dress."

How wonderful. Unlucky and also dressed as... Maria.

"Don't worry, I'll just dry my hair."

"Yes, oh well, you dry your hair and I'll fetch you a dress."

Quiet living.

Lucky for me she returned to the bathroom, which she entered regardless of the fact that I might be undressed, with a sweatshirt that must have belonged to Lorenzo. I assumed it was a piece of clothing from when he was a boy that Maria still kept in what was once her bedroom.

With dry clothes and hair, I joined the others who in the meantime had taken their seats in the dining room.

The dinner went by quietly, the table was set with two plates, a glass for water and one for wine. The bread was contained in a pretty white ceramic bowl with a decorated border, all resting on a white cotton tablecloth with an embroidered hem. The food was hearty and diverse, like every time the Ferrettis invited us to dinner. Once again it felt like being at a wedding reception. We talked about this and that. Bruno, Lorenzo's father, who is not a man of many words, just followed the conversation by moving his head to show his opinion in favor or against what we were saying. Maria, as always, was the conductor of the conversation, while Lorenzo and I joined in when she had to take a breath or fill her mouth.

That evening, in a rare moment of silence, Lorenzo spoke without being questioned by his mother. "We're planning to take a trip to Europe," he said, taking a spoonful of soup to his mouth.

I looked at him wide-eyed, amazed, actually astonished. I never would have thought that he had taken that proposal seriously, since it was not even a real one.

"Really? When?" his mother gasped enthusiastically.

"We'll think about it when Anna gets back from Myanmar."

"From Mia ... what? How is it that you always go to places nobody has ever heard of?"

"If they weren't relatively unknown, it would be useless to introduce people to them, even if this is not the case. Myanmar is quite beaten by tourism these days, it will be hard to find places that are still unexplored."

Ignoring my answer, Maria turned to us with a big, huge smile and, clapping her hands like a child, exulted: "You will finally give me a grandchild!"

Silence fell on that table set for a party, and for a moment I had the impression that we all wanted to pretend not to have heard it.

"Enough with it, Maria, you can't meddle with these things. It's their business", intervened my father-in-law, who was always ready and capable to curb his vife's enthusiasm. This time I didn't blame him.

"What do you want? They are always busy, when will they have time to have a child? If they've chosen to leave together, for once, that must be the reason!"

"Why do you think they can't have a child at home? Do they need to take a plane?"

They talked about us as if we weren't in the room. I followed that absurd exchange of opinions with a mounting anger and the desire to get up from the table and leave.

Bruno, too, must have been tired of his wife's years of insistence on the subject, because I had never seen get angry with her like that before our evening together.

I glanced at Lorenzo to urge him to put an end to that madness. It didn't bother me that there was talk of the possibility of having a child, but it was a delicate and above all private subject, which had to be treated with the respect it deserved.

"We won't have any children, Mom, I already told you, make peace with it." Those words rang in my ears. I had never heard them uttered by my husband before and they hit me like a ton of bricks and hurt me.

He had told his mother and had not told me about it.

"Anna, is this true? Why, for God's sake, don't you want to be a mom? I know it's scary but look, when you get old, you'll regret not having experienced it."

"To tell you the truth…"

"Enough, mom, leave her alone, it's none of your business" said Lorenzo interrupting my answer and putting an end to the discussion without giving further explanations. My mind was in total confusion. I watched Lorenzo go on eating without even bothering to look at me, as if what had just come to light were something obvious and well-known to everyone at that table. I was angry, indeed I was furious and, for a moment, I had the impulse to tell him that I did not agree and that the decision was not just up to him.

But I didn't speak, I stared at my dinner, which I no longer felt like eating, and let the conversation take its course. I just shook my head if I was asked a question, wishing only to leave.

While Maria was making coffee, I went to the French window that overlooked the driveway. The storm had blown away and there was only a light drizzle left to wet the asphalt.

"It seems the rain has stopped, I better take the opportunity to leave now, before it starts again."

Lorenzo used to spend time playing chess with his father after dinner. It was a moment that I did not love very much because I was kidnapped by Maria, who gave me a rundown of the town gossip she had heard here and there and that was passed from mouth to mouth so many times that it got transformed from little anecdotes to absurd tales.

Luckily we took separate cars that night and I could bail.

Once I got home, I lit the fireplace and sat down in the armchair.

I wanted to wait for Lorenzo and address the topic with him, I needed explanations but above all I needed to hear if he really meant what he had said to Maria directly from his mouth. Had he decided that we would not have children now or ever?

I was tense and struggling to sit up, even the flames in the fireplace didn't help to calm me down that evening. I got up and went into the kitchen, grabbed a glass and poured some red wine, maybe that would ease the tension. I sat down again in front of the fireplace and, with every sip, I felt the anger go away, leaving room for memories. Without haste I tried to retrace our history thinking about how we had got to that moment. I remembered that both Lorenzo and I were determined to have children immediately after getting married, but times were not good. At first he had wanted to make sure he'd established himself as a doctor in order to support our family, then we had decided to buy a bigger house. Once we found it, we started trying. Without making too many calculations, we made love "without precautions", we indulged the odds that at that moment did not seem in our favor. I did not feel the pressure of having to succeed immediately and I lived those months of planning for a new future with ease, when Angelo's proposal arrived. It was a fantastic opportunity for me and I could not have missed it, but at the same time I understood that I would not be able to ask for maternity leave right away. So we had decided to suspend our attempts at conception until I was fully integrated in my new job. However, the adjustment period to a profession that led me to travel frequently and for long periods of time had been longer than I expected. In the meantime Lorenzo had opened his clinic which kept him busy for many hours of the day. Thus, in those five years since then, we hadn't followed up on the subject of "children". Yet, my desire had not changed, on the contrary, for some time I had found myself thinking that, now that our lives were running on the tracks we had chosen, the right time had come to think about a child. Despite this, however, I had never taken the initiative to talk about it with him. It was as if every time the opportunity presented itself, something inside me told me it was not the right time.

Suddenly a heavy sadness enveloped me. I felt a heat in my chest that made its way down until it started burning in the pit of my stomach. I thought it was the wine's fault but, placing the glass on the ground, I dropped my head in my hands and burst into tears.

It was anger, disappointment, despair and fear that came out of my body after being held in for a long, long time. Crying, I felt the weight lighten until it almost disappeared and, when I calmed down, I managed to take long breaths, as if to give air to a place inside me that had been shut down for a long time. I was exhausted, all that crying had worn me out. Cocooned by the warmth of the fire I felt on my cheeks, I abandoned myself in the armchair and closed my eyes.

Suddenly I felt cold, I woke up and saw that the fireplace had gone out, my hands were frozen and my head was beating like a drum. How long had I slept? Five minutes? One hour? I got up to go to bed wondering if Lorenzo was already under the covers, but when I entered the room I didn't see him. I checked the time, it was one o'clock. I wondered if he was still out to avoid an argument with me and he probably was. I went to bed setting the alarm for five, for a day in the mountains that I didn't want to go to, but our friends had insisted on showing us their new chalet. I hated skiing and fell asleep thinking that at least I would drink some excellent hot chocolate at the cabin.

The sun lit up the room and I saw that Lorenzo was no longer in bed, turning to the bedside table to look at the time I felt my muscles already sore from the day spent in the snow. Although reluctant, they eventually convinced me to ski, which was good because I had enjoyed it like I hadn't in a long time. At the end of the day I was relaxed. The fatigue, cold and laughter had really dissolved the tension better than the wine.

When I got home I didn't want to leave that quiet state, so I avoided the topic of the previous day. For that reason, after a cup of hot tea, I went straight to sleep.

I looked at the clock placed on the bedside table, twelve past nine, I had had a decent night sleep.

I got up and looked for Lorenzo in the kitchen, then in the living room and finally in the bathroom, with no trace of him anywhere. I looked out the window and saw the dry gravel shape in the place where he had parked his car the previous evening. While I was making the coffee I noticed that there were no cups in the sink so Lorenzo had surely gone out before breakfast. I tried to remember if he had said anything to me about some engagement that morning, but nothing came to mind. It was Sunday and the next day he was leaving for London. I thought he still wanted to avoid dealing with what we had left unfinished, but then I realized that it would be too childish of him, that it did not sound like him.

I turned on my cell phone, no new messages. Eventually I decided to get dressed and get some things ready for my departure, which would be after only four days.

Within a couple of hours I had cleaned most of the house and was finishing the sleeping area when, hearing pots and pans banging, I went to the kitchen. Lorenzo was in there.

"Good morning," I said, looking at him questioningly. "I didn't hear you come in."

"Morning, since you were cleaning the rooms, I

came in to make lunch." He replied, indifferent as always.

"Where were you this morning?"

"At the clinic."

Obviously! Stupid of me for thinking otherwise.

"Did you tell me and I forgot?"

"No, I decided at the last minute but you were asleep and I didn't want to wake you. I was going to call you but time slipped by."

"All right, I'll finish cleaning up our room and I'll come to set the table, it will take ten minutes."

When I returned to the kitchen everything was ready and all I had to do was sit down at the table. Lorenzo poured some white wine into my glass first and then into his and, after taking a sip, he took the plates and brought them back to the table full of pasta with pesto and baked cherry tomatoes.

I hesitated for the duration of the lunch, I wanted to address the subject, but at the same time I was no longer moved by the anger and disappointment of two evenings before. I was just afraid, scared of being told that it was true, that his decision had been made. I was not ready to give up the idea of being a mother.

I told myself that we should discuss the matter more calmly, once we returned from our respective travels, without the anxiety of arguing, and perhaps even fighting, before being separated for a month. Thus, as with every past occasion, the topic remained in the air, silent but cumbersome.

Lorenzo told me that his flight was at six a.m. the following day, hence he would leave home in the middle of the night. He would have to pack a couple of things and then he would be free until bedtime, possibly an early one.

At about five p.m. we were both in the living room,

him sitting on the sofa leafing through a medical magazine and I in the chair with my new book in my hands. I had already reread the first five lines of the chapter three times but I couldn't grasp any of those words. I closed the book and looked up at Lorenzo. It had been fourteen years since we first met and nine years since our wedding, yet he didn't seem to have changed at all. The clean and tidy face, no beard, short hair always the same length as then, full of gel to keep them groomed. He was tall and slender, thin but not skeletal and had a proud look that, even then, gave him a serious and responsible air, giving the impression that he was a trustworthy man. That was indeed the case: I had always trusted him and I was sure I was not wrong. Although his work led him to deal with women of all kinds, eager to show him their "gratitude", I never had any doubts. My husband is a man whose word and values are more important than his own existence. He would never compromise his moral integrity as well as his professional image. A man all in one piece, as they say, who never breaks down. Not out of anger, but not out of love or passion either.

I used to find it funny when he came to pick me up at my parents' house, for example, and I jumped on his neck like a little girl. He would turn all red and say something like: "Thank you, Anna, I'm happy to see you too."

I also found him sweet because, despite his embarrassment, he had never asked me not to. Things had changed after the wedding. His responses to my displays of affection had become: "Don't get too excited" or "Don't be outrageous".

Over time I had felt more and more inappropriate and had learned to become more composed.

"Is what you told your mother true?" The words came out of my mouth without my commanding them. Lorenzo fixed his gaze on the magazine, without batting an eye. For a moment I wondered if I had uttered them, or if they were echoing in my head as they often had been since last Friday night.

The absence of an answer unnerved me and I pressed on asking him if he had heard me.

Without taking his eyes off what he was reading he replied: "I heard you."

"Why won't you answer me then?"

"I don't want to do that, actually," he said, looking at me.

"I need to know," I replied, keeping my eyes fixed on his.

"I don't think it's the right time to address this."

"Just tell me why you told her."

"I told her because otherwise she wouldn't have left me alone."

"So you don't really meant it?"

"I'm telling you, Anna, we're not going to discuss it now."

"I think that's already an answer."

After all, if the reason was to silence his mother, it would have been easy to tell me without fear of sparking an argument.

He didn't answer, so I pressed on: "Am I wrong?"

"Why are you pushing this?" he asked with an exasperated expression.

"Because I need to know now."

Lorenzo sighed, closed the magazine and, with a movement that seemed to be in slow motion, placed it on the table in front of him.

"Okay, let's talk about it, then," he agreed, settling back on the sofa with his palms resting on his thighs.

No need to argue, I just want to know if you really
ık you don't want to have children."

"I thought it would be the same for you by now."

"I'm thirty-two, I think I can still keep that door open," I replied annoyed at his statement. "Why did you think that?"

"We haven't talked about it for a long time, our lives have taken good paths. It seems to me that things are working as they are and I thought you didn't feel the need them for as well anymore."

Need... that word bothered me more than his passive attitude.

"I don't think I've ever *needed them*. It was a desire then, as it is now. I thought we both wanted them. Are you telling me it's not like that? That you don't want a kid anymore?"

"As I mentioned before, I thought we were fine the way we are."

"Answer me, for God's sake! Yes or no?" I lost my temper and those words came out at a much higher volume than I expected.

He looked at me, bothered by my rush of anger, and I knew I wasn't going to get a response because of my aggressive tone. But something inside me was bubbling and fighting to get out so, regardless of the consequences, I went on with the same rage: "You're not the only one who can make that decision, do you understand? We have to talk about it and confront each other, it's not your job, this is your marriage, and you're not the only one making choices in this house."

As expected Lorenzo did not get upset, leaving me alone in that momentary madness. He was so still it looked like he was not even breathing.

"If you love me, you have to give me an answer" I

concluded.

"Have you turned to moral blackmail now?" Is that the next step? Threatening to leave?"

"I'll do it when I realize I'm living in a marriage where I'm not valued." I was angry and realized I had never said such a thing before. At the same time, in that instant I realized that I really meant it.

"This is the reason why I didn't want to talk about it now, even though I certainly didn't expect such a scene, I understand that pre-departure stress does not allow for a reasonable discussion."

"Reasonable? So, in your opinion, it's reasonable that I should find out that you told your mother you didn't want children without ever talking about it with me first?"

"You haven't asked me again either."

"So that's it? You don't want them?"

"Yes, it is."

"Now or not even in the future?"

"I don't want them, now or ever."

There they were, the words I longed to hear.

He said it, now what? What are you going to do, Anna? How do we move forward from here?

I hadn't thought about it, I was so determined to get an answer that I didn't wonder what I would do if it ended up being true.

I remained motionless, my gaze on him but staring into space, no emotion showed me the direction to follow, only a voice in my head repeating: what now?

I took a breath and was only able to say a few words: "That's not my choice and I don't know if I can accept yours."

Then I got up from the chair and left the room, leaving him sitting on the sofa with his hands on his lap, in the same position he had kept throughout the argument.

That night Lorenzo did not sleep in our bed, he stayed - I imagined - on the sofa enough to get some rest. Then I heard him take his bags and leave the house.

I was sorry we had left it like that, but I was still too disappointed to pretend that it could end peacefully.

Over the next few days, I made the final preparations for the trip, thinking about how I could handle the subject without arguing again, but making sure that he understood that his position represented a huge obstacle to our future life together.

We spoke no more than a couple of times during his stay in London. He was very busy, indeed, and that gave me time to think for a few more days before resuming the conversation on the evening of his return. Which was also the last one before my trip.

On Wednesday in the early afternoon I was at the computer to finalize my online check-in, I would leave Milan the following morning and have a layover in London, then fly directly to Bangkok and, at the Thai dawn of my second day on the road, I'd take the Bangkok-Yangon. I heard the phone ring.

Looking at the display, I was amazed to see Lorenzo's name, who, by then, must have already been on his flight to Milan.

"Hi, haven't you left yet?"

"They canceled my flight, I'm looking for another one because the one they offered would leave late tonight."

"Wow, did you find anything?" I asked him, sorry for that inconvenience.

"Yes, but it's a flight with a layover and the result would be the same, I'd still get home tonight."

"What are you going to do?" I asked as I was selecting my seat for my London-Bangkok flight.

"I don't know, in any case I'm afraid we won't be able to see each other today."

"I understand. Okay, well, let me know if there's any news."

When I got out of bed to get ready for my departure, Lorenzo had not yet returned. The airline had offered him the night in the airport hotel because eventually, even the evening flight had been severely delayed. At that point he had preferred to leave the following morning and then head directly to the office.

I flew over the Alps thinking that Lorenzo was taking the opposite route and that, in the end, we hadn't even managed to meet halfway.

I concluded that after all he had been right: there was no need to address the subject before separating for a long time.

I wondered when and how we would talk about it again.

5

"There's something you're not telling me." Lorenzo had frightened eyes as he spoke to me, standing in front of the entrance and blocking me in.
"Nonsense, let me out or I'll miss the plane."
"When will you be back?"
"You know very well, I'll be back before Christmas." My tone of voice was annoyed and I felt impatient to leave that house.

Lorenzo moved away allowing me to cross the threshold; as soon as I was out, with his eyes fixed on his shoes and a faint voice, he said: "I know you won't be back." He closed the door and I stood motionless for a moment realizing that I had really done it. I had escaped from those walls, from that life and, as Lorenzo had already realized, I would never return. I tried to listen, inside of me, where the emotions were manifesting: my heart was beating like a drum as if it wanted to come out of my chest, my stomach had a storm of butterflies, while my mind was projecting images of my new life, alone, free, free to choose my future, free from feeling *guilty, from fears, from rules enforced by others. I felt the adrenaline rise and a lump in my throat that suddenly melted into a gigantic, really loud laugh.*

Suddenly the noise of that joy turned into music, a light, dancing music, with flutes and violins in a harmony of sounds that filled the room... room... which room? I was in a room and the noise I heard was less sweet, it was no longer music, it was irritating.

Light flooded my eyes and I recognized the sound of the alarm clock. I sat on the bed dazed, the dream was still vivid but the awareness of reality had got to me. It took me a few minutes to leave my dream world and realize that everything was absolutely normal: I was in our king bed in our room, the alarm clock was ringing annoyingly and the sound of pots and the smell of bacon came from the kitchen. All normal, except that the other half of the bed was intact.

Lorenzo did not sleep here last night.

I tried to reconstruct the events of the previous evening, I got home around eleven after dinner with Lisa, Lorenzo was in the living room reading. I stopped by to say hello before going to sleep and he told me he was going to watch a movie because he wasn't sleepy.

Had he fallen asleep on the sofa? Possible but unlikely, Lorenzo is certainly not the type who sleeps on the sofa, he never did except the night before the trip to London, but we had argued and it was a few hours' nap, he didn't even put on his pajamas.

I would have understood better by having breakfast with him.

Those were days of tension at home, certainly the argument we had had about my work had to do with it and the fact that, after more than a week, Lorenzo hadn't asked me anything about it made me very upset. It all added up to the already serious, unresolved situation of deciding not to have children. Yet, he was usually quite capable of behaving as if everything was going well, even if there were outstanding issues, but this time he wasn't and I wondered why. This destabilized me because it was an aspect of him that I didn't know how to manage. As a result, I spent more time in the bathroom than usual before joining him in the kitchen.

Lorenzo was already seated in front of a rather inviting plate of bacon and eggs. I greeted him in a low voice.

"There are more eggs if you like. And I started heating some bread", he said, keeping his eyes on the cup of coffee he was filling.

"Thanks, I think I'll use the egg to make pancakes."

"You and your sweet breakfasts," he admonished me, smiling.

Sitting down at the table after a few minutes with my nice plate of pancakes and a bottle of maple syrup, I smiled at him with an unusual serenity in my body.

"Where did you sleep? Your side of the bed was intact."

"I slept in the living room, on the sofa bed."

The sofa bed? I didn't even remember that our couch was convertible into a bed.

"You sleeping on the sofa bed? Is there something you're not telling me?"

As soon as I said those last words I smiled thinking that they were the same ones he had told me in my early morning dream.

"I wanted to read and I couldn't keep the light on in the room. As I told you last night, I wasn't sleepy."

Nothing unusual in the way we were conversing

at the table, but that morning I felt annoyed by our detached behavior. We were husband and wife, yet we chatted like two strangers who happened to be at the same bar. Was I settling for living in an emotionless marriage?

"While you were traveling I had a lot of time to think about the possibility of having a child and I did. I've come to a conclusion and I'd like to tell you about it." Lorenzo broke the silence by capturing my full attention with those words. He kept his eyes on his breakfast and this time I knew he was doing it because he found it difficult to hold my gaze.

"Tell me, I'm listening."

"I tried to imagine myself as a father, to picture what our life would be like with a child and it scares me a lot. I tried to tell myself that, at my age, it's normal to be afraid of such a radical change but that it might be worth it. Then I thought about you wanting it and I know it, even if you haven't talked about it anymore, I know you really want it. I told myself that I could not deprive you of something as important as motherhood and that you would certainly suffer from it." He paused to catch his breath and went on, I stood still as if someone had pressed pause on myself.

"The problem is…" He stared at me for a moment but immediately looked away and stared out the window. "… That is the only reason why I tried to question my decision. Your well being and your happiness. I've come to the conclusion that it is not a sufficient reason."

I watched him fiddle with his fork on his plate as his vulnerability overcame his armor of pride and rigor. He looked helpless and worried. I also had the feeling that there was more.

"Are you telling me that you've thought about it

and that you've understood that there is no place for a child in your life?" I asked him in a gentle and condescending tone.

He just nodded.

"Is that all you want to tell me?"

Lorenzo looked at me with a surprised air, but then, still without making a sound, he shook his head again to confirm.

I sighed. "Thanks for being honest."

"I know it's not enough for you, though," he said, his voice shaking.

I looked down this time as he turned to me.

"I don't know if it is." It wasn't. Plus, I felt that the confession came too late, but I was still grateful to find myself in front of an honest man who had opened his heart as, perhaps, never before.

"I understand... take your time."

With some amazement at the sensitivity he was showing, I nodded as he had done a little while before and, in gratitude, smiled at him.

Something in his attitude had changed. His openness to me could be something positive for our relationship. At the same time, however, it seemed strange and unnatural to me.

6

The phone was ringing relentlessly, but since I was in the shower I tried to ignore it. To no avail because with each ring my shoulders contracted in an irritating tension. I gave up and chose to go out. I took out my cell phone, which in the meantime had stopped ringing, and saw three missed calls on the display. Enough time for me to dry my hands to unlock the screen, and again the phone rang. The caller was unknown.

"Hello?" I said, uncertain whether I was right to answer.

On the other hand of the line, the familiar and unexpected voice of Giorgia, Angelo's secretary, replied with the tone of someone in a hurry: "Hello, sorry if I've called you a thousand times."

"No, no worries, I'm sorry I didn't pick up, I was in the shower."

"I wanted to know if we can meet for a coffee, I need to talk to you."

Giorgia was a nice girl with whom I had, over time,

exchanged chitchat and laughter, but we didn't have the bond that justified a sudden conversation over coffee. My mind started building the castle of anxieties and fears about my job again.

"Yes, gladly, tell me when you are free." I didn't want to worry any more, so I didn't ask her what she had to talk to me about so urgently.

"I'd be free now if you could meet. If there is a bar near you, I can join you there."

It was definitely worth getting antsy.

"Listen, I'm home alone, is it okay if I make you some coffee here?"

"Sounds like a great idea to me. Thanks for your time."

"No problem, do you know where I live?"

"No, I actually don't." She actually seemed upset.

"I'll send you the address, okay?"

"Okay, thanks, see you later."

I finished drying myself off and got dressed trying to stay calm, I went to the kitchen to make coffee while my heart seemed to want to pop out of my chest. I wondered if chamomile tea would be a better option.

There were a thousand reasons why Giorgia might have needed to talk to me, I began to think, but it wasn't like that and I knew it well.

Maybe she's pregnant and doesn't know how to tell Angelo, or she doesn't know how to tell her boyfriend... no, no ... that would mean she didn't even have a friend, for her to come and ask me for advice on how to tell her boyfriend. Okay, maybe it's the first one, she's pregnant and doesn't know how to tell Angelo. That's plausible.

When Giorgia entered the house she seemed embarrassed, perhaps for having turned in like this, without explanation. Or maybe because she had to give me some bad news? I tried to stay calm and show as much hospitality as possible.

"Come on, have a seat, I've made some coffee, let's go to the kitchen."

"Thanks again, Anna, you don't know how stupid I feel for bothering you like this. Ah, here, I brought some croissants."

"Well, croissants are already a good reason to be here." We both tried to get rid of the embarrassment, she smiled and followed me into the kitchen.

I saw her having a hard time talking about what was troubling her so, once were seated and with cups full of steaming black coffee, I encouraged her to get started. "Tell me, what happened?"

She gave me a tight smile, like a parent who is about to give their child bitter medicine but wants them to believe it will be a good experience.

"I wanted to ask you why Angelo canceled all the trips you had planned for the next few months."

Here was a question that already opened new scenarios, the worst ones.

"What do you mean he cancelled them?" I asked after taking a deep breath.

"While you were in Myanmar he gave me the list of your upcoming trips, he told me to enter them in the database and send them to him by e-mail on your return so that he could offered them to you." She took a sip of coffee, I followed the movement with my eyes. "When you came to the office last time, I sent him the e-mail as per his request. But in the afternoon, after you were gone, he replied telling me to cancel them all. I just wanted to ask you why, if I'm not too indiscreet."

This was really absurd, Angelo had played a part, pretending to be serene as if everything were absolutely normal. So what? Was my hunch right? I wasn't sure yet, but everything pointed in that direction.

Showing my astonishment about her story, I talked to her about how things had gone that day, I told her that I knew nothing about the trips scheduled and later canceled and that at the moment Angelo had benched me "just" until October.

"However, I can't hide from you that since that day I have often thought about Angelo's decision with a certain fear. Listen, Giorgia, why did you come here to ask me this? I mean, I guess it's not just because you're worried about me, right?"

She took a deep breath as if to find the courage. "There have been a lot of meetings between members in the last period, about two a week. At first I was trying to think that everything was okay, but the other day I couldn't take it anymore and I did a horrible thing. If they found out I would be fired on the spot."

"What did you do?"

"I used the internal phone line to listen to their meeting," she said guiltily, looking down. I stared at her as if she were a UFO. I would never have been able to do such a thing, maybe not even think about it, it was brilliant!

"And what did you hear?"

"I distinctly heard that Angelo is out of the company."

My eyes widened. "Angelo?! But how? Can they do this?"

She shrugged, spreading her hands. "They told him that we need to cut expenses, change some things in the magazine and that, according to them, our environment was too 'homely'. They want to look for people who can report for free, only paying for travel, food and accommodation expenses but without paying a commission on the material. They say there is a line of people who would like to do it. I have been trying to find more information for days but no one in the newsroom is talking about it, in fact I think I'm the only one who knows. In addition to Angelo, of course, but he too acts as if nothing's happened. So I thought maybe he had said something to you that day, to justify all those canceled trips. But now I understand that you too were unaware of it."

I was upset, much worse than I thought. I was afraid for my place in favor of the newcomers... instead we would all have been thrown out to make room for strangers without a shred of competence.

I dropped back onto the back of the chair, staring off into space. I listened to my body realize that it was all true, that my thoughts were reality and that soon what I feared would actually happen.

I raised my head and saw Giorgia in front of me with my same resignation on her face, I understood that she too was worried about her job and beyond that, she was sorry to think about that welcoming and warm environment soon becoming just a memory.

I asked her if she could find out how soon the company would make the changes. She replied that she did not know but that my travels weren't the only ones that had been canceled and colleagues were starting to wonder what they would publish in the magazine in a few months, when the material was finished. Without new trips there would have been no articles to write, anyone would have understood this.

I asked her if she was going to do anything but she told me she had no idea what to do. I agreed with her.

"Perhaps the only thing that really makes sense is to start looking for another job," she concluded resignation marring her face.

When she left, I stayed in the house for several hours thinking about everything we had said to each other. I tried to imagine what was going to happen to the editorial office and, of course, to my job. I had to start over, it scared me.

Too many things were changing, the cornerstones of my life were compromised: I no longer recognized Lorenzo, or perhaps I was realizing that I had never really known him, the idea of family that I had always carried in my heart was no longer an option and the job I loved so much was disappearing in a cloud of smoke. I felt like a juggler and didn't understand if it made sense to try to keep the game on its feet or to let it all fall apart.

I called Lisa, but the answering machine went off so I left her a message saying I needed to see her, then I decided to go for a swim in the pool to momentarily get away from that flurry of thoughts.

The water was perfect, at twenty-seven degrees, and swimming was pleasant even though I hated the cap that squeezed my temples. When I went out I felt lighter and more relaxed. After the shower, after drying my hair, I looked at the phone I had left in the locker along with my clothes and saw that Lisa had called me twice. I got dressed and, as soon as I got into the car, I called her back.

"Finally! Where were you? I have great news for you." I got the impression that she hadn't heard my message.

"I was in the pool, I'm all ears," I replied intrigued by her enthusiasm.

"Do you remember I told you about a trip to Spain?" Without letting me answer, she went on: "Well, I'm leaving on Thursday and you're coming with me!"

"What do you mean?" I asked her bewildered.

"I have to support a client in a real estate auction and, since they practically forced me to go, I said I would bring a friend, so on Thursday and Friday I will be busy with my client but, if we come back on Sunday, we can enjoy two days in Barcelona."

I was silent for a moment thinking about her proposal which in fact, at that moment, was not bad at all.

"Sounds like a great plan," I replied.

Lisa was elated and her enthusiasm infected me too, for the first time in weeks I felt really excited about something.

She told me that I had to send her the details of my ID card because her law firm would pay for the flight and the hotel and that she would then send me every detail by e-mail.

It was already Tuesday, we would be leaving after only two days. I had to tell Lorenzo, but that didn't bother me.

At home I prepared the pizza dough I was going to cook for dinner, it had to rest for a couple of hours and I took the opportunity to go and inspect my wardrobe. In fact, I was not used to taking "recreational" trips, usually my travel clothing included two pairs of long and wide trousers, one light and one dark-which could be transformed into summer shorts by detaching the fabric from the thigh to the ankle-, white short sleeved t-shirts, a gray hooded sweatshirt, a beige turtleneck sweater and sneakers. All almost useless for walking on the streets of Barcelona with a friend. Certainly I could find something from the "good clothes" wardrobe. There was an emerald green dress with small white flowers that I really liked and that I hardly ever wore. The skirt was neither too short nor too long. I needed to find something elegant to wear on weekend evenings, but searching harder I'd surely find it. I'm certainly not the person to be put off by some missing piece of clothing.

I enjoyed organizing my suitcase mentally, I probably hadn't been on a trip with a friend since graduation. Between one dress and the next I felt the weight of the news that Giorgia had brought me for breakfast, but at that moment I didn't want to spoil my mood and, shrugging my shoulders, I acted as if I wanted to shake it off.

The oven timer brought me back to reality, so I abandoned the selection of clothes to go back to devoting myself to pizza.

When Lorenzo opened the door it was almost eight and dinner would be ready in minutes.

He came into the kitchen to greet me and then disappeared into the sleeping area. I set the table, took the pizzas out of the oven and put the hot pans on the counter.

I had several things to talk to him about: Giorgia's visit in the morning and the pleasant surprise that Lisa had given me. I didn't know what to start with, but still not wanting to let go of the wave of excitement I was riding, I decided to talk to him about Lisa's call. Lorenzo seemed not only amazed, but almost worried. He was visibly uncomfortable, and if I hadn't known him so well, I would have thought I also saw some signs of anxiety in his behavior. I lingered asking him if the proposition upset him.

"It just seems strange to me that Lisa invited a friend on a business trip," she replied, giving me the impression that he was repressing an emotion.

"Lisa knows I have a lot of worries these days, I think she did it to distract me a bit. Besides, she didn't want to go alone, she already told me some time ago."

"What thoughts are you talking about?" he asked me looking up in what seemed like a panic. Obviously he must have known what thoughts were tormenting me, but then I realized he was worried about something else. That is, me telling Lisa about our problems. Lorenzo had grown up under the banner of "washing one's dirty clothes at home", and perhaps he hoped that I would not even talk to my best friend.

"I guess you know what my thoughts are right now, and about that... there's one more thing I need to tell you."

"Tell me," he encouraged me, pouring me a drink.

"This morning Angelo's secretary came to see me. She was very upset about what she found out in the office."

I told him the whole conversation I had in our house without leaving out any details. I also told him about the way Giorgia had obtained the information even though I knew he would not approve of it, but it was important that he understood that the source was reliable. He followed my story carefully until I stopped talking.

"Well, you were right, you had seen it right," he exclaimed, holding the knife to cut a piece of pizza. "I'm sorry to hear that."

"The thing is, I'm out of a job now, and I have to start looking for something."

"It's not official yet, if Angelo hasn't talked about it with his employees, maybe he has something in mind to save you all. Haven't you thought about it?"

Truthfully no, I hadn't, but at that moment it didn't seem like a good idea to hold on to in hopes of not losing my job.

"Anyway, keeping your options open is not a bad thing, you might even find a job that you like better, after all you haven't had other real experiences besides being part of Angelo's editorial staff."

This was also true, but if I had never thought of anything else, it was because I was comfortable where I was. I accepted Lorenzo's suggestions, thanking him for giving me his point of view. He then asked me other questions about the weekend in Barcelona. His tone was soft and he seemed less worried, especially after learning about the negative side of my day as well. I appreciated him changing his tone and the interest he paid to… me. I still didn't know what our future would be like, I didn't know if I would feel what we had was enough by having to give up the idea of a child, and I didn't even know if and how long that reconciliation would last. However, I appreciated him and in that moment, without the desire of tilting at windmills, it was enough.

Later in bed, while I was reading, I felt cold; I got up and went to get a woolen blanket from the closet and, as soon as I put it on, my body relaxed, wrapped in that warmth. I fell asleep like that, with a book in my hands and the lamp on.

7

The morning after, upon waking up, I found the closed book on the bedside table with its bookmark sticking out a few pages from the end of the volume. The wool blanket still kept me warm and to my left the bed was already empty. Lorenzo had just got up because I could hear him in the bathroom.

"Good morning," I said, trying to get my voice heard from the other side of the closed door. No reply.

I heard the faucet turn off and seconds later he walked out of the bathroom. "Ah, you're awake, good morning."

"Morning."

"You fell asleep while reading last night, your book must not be that exciting." He was smiling and seemed to be in a good mood.

"The book is nice, but I was tired and relaxed too much in the warmth of the blankets."

"Good for you, you'll be well rested today. Speaking

of that, you will have many things to do."

I nodded, mentally going over the list of things that I had started visualizing the day before and which began with "send documents to Lisa".

Damn! The documents! I haven't sent her the email yet.

I jumped out of bed and hurried to turn on my cell phone. In the meantime, I took the wallet from my purse and extracted my identity card. As soon as the phone lit up, I dialed the unlock code and photographed the front and back of the document.

I immediately sent the email with the attachment apologizing for the delay.

Having settled the matter of the documents I could start the day of preparations.

By lunchtime I had already done most of the work, finding everything I needed in the closet to fill my suitcase. I just had to go to the library to look for a new book in which to immerse myself during those few days abroad. I thought that maybe I wouldn't get to read having a friend with me, but leaving without a new book in my bag gave me that unpleasant feeling of having forgotten something important at home.

I received a message from Lisa telling me that a car would come to my house at eight the next day and, after picking her up, it would take us to the airport two hours early.

I thought that with the hand luggage and the check-ins already done being so early was an excess of caution, but then I considered that, being Lisa a famous latecomer, that precaution was probably not wrong.

Thinking about dinner, I wanted to prepare something different from usual for Lorenzo and me. Romantic? Perhaps.

On the way home I stopped at the grocery store to buy what I needed, added a bottle of Amarone and a bouquet of fragrant flowers, bought from the florist next door. The positive energy of that weekend abroad was bursting into my daily life like a ray of sunshine entering a dark room.

Later, while the lasagna was cooking in the oven, the shower made me think about Giorgia again, the future prospects of my work. Worry was contrasted with something new, something uplifting. Hot water poured over my skin, taking away tension and worries. Suddenly I stopped as if struck by an image. It was me, writing an article in Spanish on the computer in an office overlooking the sea.

A thought as strong as a memory, real, detailed.

I found myself laughing alone under the stream of water thinking of my poor mind which, now overloaded, was creating absurd images, randomly mixing the amount of information it had received in that last period.

That evening - which began with a well-set table, a perfectly successful steaming lasagna and a red wine that warmed the soul - passed lightly. At home there was a new atmosphere, sparkling like the first evenings of summer when you're back to dining outdoors and it's still light outside, the air is no longer cold but still not hot and everything is... simply enjoyable.

Lorenzo and I chatted intoxicated by that feeling of peace and, as if neither of us wanted to lose that moment of newfound complicity, we continued the evening in the living room. Lorenzo lit the fire and I uncorked the second bottle of wine. How easy it was to talk about everything, how easy it was to be together that evening. Why was I convinced it was difficult? Even impossible now? Was I wrong?

Had I raised the wall between us, and had he only leaned on it? Perhaps if I had relaxed a little, he too would have let his guard down.

It was thanks to that newfound harmony, and undoubtedly the good *Amarone* and the warmth of the flames that crackled in the fireplace, that finally that evening Lorenzo and I made love.

It had been a long time, for sure before my last trip, before something came between us, between our intimacy, something I didn't know but that made our not loving each other seem perfectly normal.

Only that evening, while we were still lying on the bed, did I realize that there was nothing normal about not making love in a marriage. And that I didn't want to live in a loveless one.

The car Lisa had booked arrived on time. Lorenzo came to send me off at our door. With his hand on the handle he blocked the exit as he stood looking at me as I put on my coat. I immediately had the sensation of déjà-vu, we had already experienced that scene, very similarly, in my dream. For a moment I expected to hear him say the same words but I was relieved to see him approach me smiling and kissing me goodbye.

"Have fun," he told me once I was outside. As soon as he closed the door behind me, I again expected to feel that whirlwind of emotions with which that dream ended and I was amazed to realize that instead… I felt nothing. No disruptive enthusiasm, no search for a new freedom, no heartbeat and no expectation. I was serene.

After about three hours, sitting on the plane in my aisle seat and with my head resting on the seat,

I thought about everything that had happened since the last time gear wheels had brought me back to the ground. That day I landed with only one thought: having to make a choice between marriage and motherhood. Now I was leaving with a thousand questions, my whole life had been turned upside down and reshuffled. No certainty, no direction to take. Only, perhaps, something to wait for, something that sooner or later would come to show me the way.

Although I continued to think about Giorgia's words, I felt calm, that tightness in my stomach I had had when leaving the office the last time and the anxiety that had accompanied me for the following days had disappeared. Perhaps having sensed what was about to happen had prepared me to better endure the blow that had come. Even if not in an official way, as Lorenzo had pointed out.

But there was something else that was helping me react so calmly. I realized that leaving with Lisa was giving me a completely different energy from any other trip. It was a new incentive that, to my surprise, was making me look at life with more optimism.

Even in the possibility of a career change, I now saw more of the opportunity for a fresh start than the fear of something ending.

8

Arriving at the hotel we immediately had the first surprise of the trip: Lisa's studio had booked two separate double rooms. Being good friends, we both imagined sharing a room but in fact, Lisa told me, she had not specified our intention to the secretary, so - as is the custom in the world of business travel - she had booked two. In the end we decided to take advantage of the magnanimity of Maggi and Fauberti law firm.

The rooms were ready and we went up to unpack. Lisa was scheduled to meet with the client at three p.m., which gave us time for a quick lunch. I grabbed the book I got from the library and put it in my backpack, I sent a message to Lorenzo to tell him that I had arrived and I went to wait for Lisa in the hotel lobby.

Outside the building we were hit by a beam of dazzling light, looking around we realized that Summer, more than Spring, seemed to have already conquered the city. It was early April and people were

already walking in short sleeves. We had d(
stay in the Barceloneta neighborhood to b(
enjoy the sea a few steps from the hotel an
same time, be comfortable in the center. Tl
at the end of the street was packed with p
bathing suits sunbathing; even if no one dared to dive
into the sea, I had the impression that was close to
happening.

Sitting at a bar with tables outside we ordered a mix of tapas and two cervezas while, between bites, we tried to plan those days. Lisa briefly told me her client's story, mostly to explain the steps that this operation involved.

"To be honest, my presence here is not essential," she pointed out, speaking of the matter. "But the fact is that this guy's mother was a loyal client of Maggi Senior, the oldest partner, and when the son called him and said he would feel more protected with a trusted attorney onsite, he couldn't find it in him to tell him no. Just think that I haven't met him in person yet."

"Sorry, and why didn't he come?" Maggi Senior, I mean."

"Because he's eighty-two," Lisa replied with an expression of feigned resignation as if to say, *"Hence, it was my turn."*

She explained that the meeting that afternoon was first of all to get to know each other and then to talk about the details of the auction set for the next day and that his client seemed determined to win. She would then go with a curator appointed by the judge to view it with the proposed buyer and a friend of the latter, who worked in real estate.

"Well, he mustn't be doing pretty well, this man."

"Well..." said Lisa, "I don't know yet if he does

nis for a living or he's doing it out of need. I'll tell you more tonight after meeting him, over a paella, maybe."

"I'm curious now, so yes to the paella."

I saw her peek at the time on the phone. "I have to go, are you coming to the center with me? I'm stopping at Plaza Catalunya."

"I think for today I will enjoy the sun on the beach, the city will not have changed too much since the last time I visited it, I can postpone the tour until tomorrow."

"Great, when I finish I'll pick you up at the hotel and take you to dinner downtown."

"Deal."

I greeted Lisa and went to my room to put on my bathing suit, within minutes I was barefoot on the sand. I laid with my belly on the towel, moving my torso left and right to shape the sand according to my body. The warmth of the sun on my shoulders was pleasant. With a movement that made me arch my back, I took the book out of my bag and started reading it.

The story won me over from the very first pages, it was about a man, husband and family man, who after years realized he had neglected his wife and their marriage, focusing only on work. He knew he had done it to ensure a good lifestyle for the family that, with three children, he had to provide for with his salary alone. But at what price? The man in the novel was starting to wonder, and I was starting to do the same, asking myself why people at some point in a relationship shift their interest outside of the couple. Of course, not all people do, but looking back on the family models that had accompanied me in life, I could not explain why many, in one way or another, had fallen into that trap. I then reflected on the fact that, as soon as the danger of losing the other became real, all those gestures and attentions put aside often reappeared and it became easy again to dedicate them to the partner. As if, at a certain point, only the fear of losing one another could awaken a sleeping love. I wondered if the same thing was also happening between me and Lorenzo. For him, his job had always required a lot of his attention and time, but in the early years he managed to give the same importance to both us and his career, a fifty-fifty, let's say. Then, over time, work had taken up more and more space, stealing it from our home life. But hadn't I done the same? Before starting to work for Angelo, I always planned trips also based on my husband's commitments, so that we didn't happen to be traveling at different times or spent too much time without seeing each other. Of course then it was easy, I was the only one to plan my trips without my time being dictated by others. Working at the newsroom, the trips were conceived according to the articles' times of release and the dates were little if not at all tractable. But the question was: had I asked myself if by doing so I was neglecting my family since then?

In the evening, sitting outdoors at the restaurant table, at what was not yet dinner time for the Spanish, we followed with our eyes the comings and goings of people who walked a few centimeters from our table, feeling part of the fun chaos that is the Rambla.

A waiter placed a jug of sangria and two glasses in front of us.

"So, tell me about the mysterious client," I said to Lisa as I wriggled in my chair looking for a position that didn't hurt my skin, a little red from the afternoon ahh, he's a nice guy! Also fascinating, I must

"Well, that never hurts. What else?"
"I haven't discovered much else, actually. He was looking for an apartment here in Barcelona. He came across the real estate auction announcement by accident and saw a good investment in it. His name is Miguel."
"What more did you have to find out?"
"Nothing else, actually."
"Have you seen the house?"
"Yes, yes, I've seen it, it needs to be redone from head to toe. But it will undoubtedly gain value once it is fixed."
"Let's have a toast to Miguel, then, thanks to him we are sitting on the Rambla drinking sangria!" I exclaimed, holding up the glass.
"He truly made a little miracle, Migueliño. Cheers!" Lisa chuckled emulating my gesture.
Wrapped in that holiday feeling, Lisa and I spent a special evening, talking and laughing as if there was nothing more important in the world than that precise moment. How long had it been since the last time the two of us alone - without time being marked by work commitments, responsibilities and duties – felt so... young?

9

The following morning the awakening was less poetic.

"Just so I'm clear," Lisa exclaimed, looking at me, "you, with such delicate skin, spent an afternoon in the sun without wearing SPF?"

I nodded sadly.

"When you travel for work they also pay for a nurse to look after you, I guess!"

"Come on, don't rub it in, I'm already humiliated enough."

"More than humiliated you are burned! Look at that back! Do you want me to ask reception to call emergency care?"

"No no, it's not that bad. Now I'll slowly get dressed and go buy an Aloe Vera cream. You'll see, I'll be better afterwards."

"I would go for you, but I have to get ready for the auction. Man, it's ten o'clock already!"

"Go go, don't worry, I've been through worse. See you later. By the way, what time will you be free?"

"It depends on how long the auction will last. In any case, when it finishes I have to come to the hotel to send some documents to the studio and do a few things. It'll take me a couple of hours."

"Okay, I'll wait for your call then."

I stayed in my room the whole morning trying to relieve the burning of my skin under the jet of the ice cold shower, but as soon as I tried to put on a shirt it felt as if a million pins were stuck in every millimeter of my back. Not to mention the bra I had by now given up.

I had no choice, even if it was painful: without a cream I would never have been able to calm the stinging, so I armed myself with courage and, in pain, I slipped into the largest shirt I had and set out in search of a sunburn cream. The sun beating down on my back increased the pain giving me the impression that my shirt was on fire.

I walked on the sidewalk looking for some shade and I realized that I was more careful to dodge the sun's rays than to look for what I had left the hotel for. I hailed a taxi and asked the driver to take me to the nearest open pharmacy as I rummaged through my bag for the phone that I felt vibrating.

"Good morning!" I said answering the call.

"Good morning, señorita, how are you doing?" Lorenzo asked.

"I've been better, I'm in a taxi looking for a pharmacy."

"What happened?"

"I got sunburnt."

"Come on! Is it so hot there?"

"Yes, yesterday I was on the beach all afternoon

and I don't know why I didn't think about putting SPF on."

"It's not like you."

"I know."

"Is it that bad?"

"I don't know if it's serious, but it hurts to death."

The street was starting to get much busier and looking around I didn't understand where we had ended up.

"Sorry, Lorenzo, I have to say goodbye because I have no idea where the taxi driver is taking me to get this cream."

"Across the city! Like all taxi drivers do with tourists."

"Ugh!" I snorted closing the call.

"Excuse me, where are we?" I tried the most Spanish pronunciation possible, but something comical came out and I laughed at myself.

The taxi driver answered me in Catalan, further mortifying me since I did not understand half a word.

It will cost me as much as last night's dinner, this journey.

In fact, I spent all the cash I had in my wallet to pay for the unsolicited sightseeing tour and, after getting dropped off at Plaza Catalunya, I looked around for my shop.

I went into a small market on the side of the road hoping to find a suitable cream there and luckily I did.

When I got to the cashier, I took my credit card from my wallet to pay, but the transaction was denied. I asked the cashier to try again but the outcome was the same. I ran out of cash and the card didn't work, I was resigned to leaving the jar of cream there when a voice coming up from behind me stopped me.

"May I pay for it?" I turned in the direction of that voice. Behind me a tall man was holding a six-pack. His delicate and regular face seemed drawn by expert hands and his eyes of an intense black made his gaze magnetic and penetrating.

I remained motionless, as if electrocuted.

"Allow me?" he pressed on.

"Eh... no, yes... that's, there is no... need. Thanks," I stammered.

The man leaned towards me and I instinctively held my breath.

"I'm afraid we are holding up the line so let's just do this: I buy your cream, then, if you like, I'll give it to you later, otherwise I'll keep it. Okay?"

He took the cream and, in fluent Catalan, told the cashier to put it in his bill. Only then did I realize that the man had spoken to me in Italian.

"I don't know how to thank you, you really shouldn't have," I told him as soon as I left the shop.

"I was three feet away from you and the heat from your back was warming my beers", he replied, laughing as he stuffed the bottles into his backpack.

My hands were sweaty and an uncontrolled shaking shook my body. I didn't have time to wonder what the hell was happening to me when he looked up at me making me hotter than the sunburn that was tormenting me.

"Can I offer you a coffee?"

I swallowed. "I should be the one offering to pay you back," I replied trying to appear as casual as possible.

"Yes, but you wouldn't know how to."

True. I could not have imagined a more embarrassing situation.

"Listen, my proposal is we go to the bar across the street, sit in the shade and you give me permission to be less formal with each other. If you say yes, we are even."

I didn't even realize I was being formal. I felt like I was hit by a car and saw fragmented and blurry images of what was happening around. "Okay," was all I could say.

"How do you get your coffee... uh?"

"My name is Anna, I'll have a regular, thank you."

As soon as I answered him, he disappeared into the room and I blew the air out of my lungs as if I had forgotten to breathe in the last ten minutes. I put down the phone which, the instant it touched the table, rang.

"Hello! The bad news is that the auction is only now over. I'm on my way to the hotel but I have to work, are you still in your room?"

"No, I'm downtown, I came to buy cream and now I'm about to have a coffee." For some reason I didn't tell her I wasn't alone.

"So I assume you're feeling better then."

"Yes, better, thanks." It wasn't true, but the heat that the man's presence caused me overwhelmed the burning of my skin, making me feel like one big bonfire.

"Well, then I'll call you when I'm done to make a plan, okay?"

"Okay, see you later. Ah no, wait..."

"What?"

"What's the good news?"

"Ah yes! My client would like to celebrate the purchase of the house and invited us to dinner. I told him I would hear from you and then I would answer him. Are you up for it?"

"Sorry, did he invite me too?"

"Sure, it's not a business dinner, his real estate friend is there too."

"I don't know, Lisa, it almost feels like a double date to me."

"It's so obvious you're used to traveling alone! Look, what if I told him to book early, like around seven? Then we'll have the rest of the evening to ourselves."

"In Spain? At seven? At that time here, if you sit down at the table, they'll still serve you cappuccino!"

"You're right. Okay, well, I'll tell him no."

I stopped for a moment to think. After all, we were in Barcelona because of that deal and perhaps Lisa would have found it useful to go.

"No, you know what? You're right, why shouldn't we accept? Please confirm. I'm coming back to the hotel to get ready soon."

"No rush! See you later, dear."

With practically perfect timing, my recent encounter returned to the table with the two coffees in hand.

Fortunately, the phone call with Lisa had brought me back down to earth and, at least for a while, I stopped acting like someone who had just seen a ghost.

But his closeness continued to upset me, as if I was no longer the master of my own body, I felt my heart beating fast, immediately afterwards a leg was jumping uncontrollably, my hands were sweating and my eyes could not support his gaze. I was sure I had never been a victim of such a sensation before. He, on the contrary, seemed calm, completely at ease in this conversation between strangers.

"Where are you from, Anna?" Just hearing him say

my name made me swallow hard.

"I'm from Milan. How about you?"

"I'm from Perugia."

"Umbria? You don't have an Umbrian accent." Not that I was an expert in accents, on the contrary, the only one I could distinguish without hesitation was the Apulian one due to the many summer holidays I had taken with my family in Salento.

"You don't have a Milanese accent either. Fortunately!" he said, accompanying the dig with a smile that I found out of this world.

"Do you think so? I think I have it all right."

"I don't know, you don't have the 'néé'!"

He made me laugh. We spent the next hour talking about ourselves. He told me he had graduated where he was now teaching, at the economics department of Perugia, and he seemed to be fascinated by what I told him about my job. In some moments, while he was speaking, I tried to study that perfect face, so expressive. I had already noticed the small wrinkles next to his eyes and now smiling he was sporting two very sweet dimples on the sides of his mouth. He had dark brown hair, long enough to curl in a slight wave, which looked super soft. I could hardly keep myself from touching them. Although I had gained the ability to raise my eyes to him as he spoke, I still could not hold his gaze. I crossed his eyes for just a moment, while I was telling him about my last trip and he was staring at me captivated by my words, and that paralysis effect stopped me again, this time to the point that he had to ask me to continue.

"Did you come here for work or pleasure?" I asked.

"Let's say a bit of both, you?" He vaguely answered.

"I'm here with a friend."

"So for fun?"

"Let's say a bit of both", I replied, enjoying the smile he gave back. I couldn't get over how the man had sent my nervous system into a tailspin. The effort I was putting into trying to look natural was unbearable and I wondered if it was at least working, or if I looked like a crazy person to him. Like when you can't laugh at something funny and holding back the muscles of your face creates absurd expressions. You don't laugh, but you don't look ok either. I noticed that I was nervously fiddling with a lock of hair and suddenly stopped doing it. In the meantime he drank his coffee quietly, with a relaxed air that made him even more fascinating.

I had the feeling that time had gone faster than I expected and, without even looking at the clock, I said to him: "It's late, I have to go back to the hotel, my friend is waiting for me." After all, what was I doing there? It had been a pleasant meeting but there was no point in extending the moment. Indeed, perhaps I should really leave.

"All right, Anna, thanks for the chat, it was fun talking to you." Again, hearing him say my name had a shattering effect on me.

"Thank you for everything, the coffee and the cream. You have been a true gentleman." I got up from my chair and he did so too, but the moment I was on my feet, suddenly my vision blurred and everything around me went out.

"Anna... Anna, can you hear me? Anna?"

The voice felt far and, although I commanded my mouth to answer, I was unable to.

"Sit down. My God, you're shaking."

Gradually the voice came closer and, just as slowly, the images around me began to take color again, and then shape.

With my vision still blurred, I caught a glimpse of him taking something out of his backpack and placing it on top of me. A blanket? I immediately felt the warmth and smiled.

"Anna, finally! You scared the hell out of me. How are you feeling?"

"I'm sorry." My voice was weak but, slowly recovering my strength, I continued: "I just realized I haven't eaten since last night."

"Are you sure it's just that? You're shivering and your skin is hot."

"Yes, I think the sunburn's not helping either."

Regaining energy I sat up in my chair, I was overwhelmed like someone who suddenly wakes up from a deep sleep.

"Get something to eat, you need it."

"Don't worry, I'm better now, plus I really have to go."

I wasn't sure what I was saying but I didn't want him to feel compelled to pay for my food too.

Regardless of my answer, he asked me if I was a vegetarian.

I was amazed by that question. How had he known?

"Yes, how do you know?"

He shrugged. "A feeling."

He ordered a veggie sandwich and a bottle of water and, while we waited for the food to be ready, he suggested I put on his sweater.

I looked down and found that it was not a blanket he had placed on me as I came to. I was reluctant but I was cold so I took his advice.

"Where are you staying?" he asked, his expression still worried.

"Hotel 54."

"But it's in Barceloneta!"

"Yup."

I thought he had to come to Barcelona often to know the city so well.

"But you can't go there alone."

"Yes I can, don't worry."

"May I take you?"

"No need, really, I'll take a taxi."

"But you can't pay for it."

"Sure I can, when I get there I'll tell my friend to come down and bring my card. No problem."

"Maybe... but I'm not very convinced." He put a hand to his forehead as if to focus more. "What if I take a taxi with you and you call your friend anyway to pay the driver?"

He understood what was holding me back from allowing him to accompany me: that man was reading me.

I thought about not giving in, but I felt pretty weak, so I accepted his offer again and, as soon as our order was ready, he stopped the first available taxi.

My head was spinning and I couldn't look out the window at the images that passed too quickly. I took a few bites of the sandwich, but with that dizziness I couldn't swallow without feeling my stomach rolling over.

"How are you feeling?" asked that man I didn't know existed until a few hours before, but who had already saved me twice.

"Not good, I can't keep my head up," I replied, this time without lying.

"Come on, lean here." He put his arm around me making me rest gently on his shoulder. Suddenly a hurricane of fragrances hit my senses: lavender, cedar, bergamot all in a single explosion of perfume. Intoxicating. With my head now abandoned on him and my eyelids so heavy I could not keep my eyes open, I sought the strength to rebel against that spell by which I had been bewitched.

"I can't do that" I said, my voice weak.

"Why?"

"I don't know who you are."

"I'm Michele."

10

"Anna... Anna... We're here."
His soft voice woke me up. Again. Opening my eyes I tried to figure out where I was. As soon as I realized I had my head on his shoulder, I straightened up too suddenly and caused a headache.
"Oh my God, I'm sorry, I'm mortified. I must have fallen asleep."
"Don't worry, how are you feeling?"
I became aware of my body and I realized that I had regained my strength. "Better, I feel rested."
"I'm glad to hear it. We're at your hotel." He pointed out the window on my side with his index finger. "Do you want me to take you inside?"
"No need, thanks."
I saw him get out of the car and thought that he still wasn't taking me seriously. Then I turned to open the door, but it swung open before I could touch it. Michele held out his hand to help me get

out of the car.

I took it. We were facing each other a few inches apart and, again, my heart began to pound in my chest. He raised his arm and with his fingers brushed a lock of hair from my face, then he touched my cheek gently. "Are you sure you're okay?"

I smiled at him and nodded. At that moment I realized I hadn't called Lisa.

"Wait, wait," I exclaimed, breaking the spell.

"What happened?"

I picked up the phone. "I'll have Lisa bring my card." He grabbed the hand I was dialing with and stopped me. "Let me at least pay for the taxi. Please," I pleaded.

"Here's the deal, if we meet again within the next few days, you'll pay for the drinks."

What if I don't see you again? I wanted to ask him. But I realized how inappropriate it was to have even thought of it… to have feared it.

"I feel like you always have an offer ready for any circumstance."

He smiled. "See you, Anna."

"Goodbye."

I stood by the side of the road for a moment, bewildered by what had just happened. The black and yellow car pulled away until it disappeared behind a building.

11

"Anna, you're pale as a ghost, what happened?"

Lisa, seeing me enter the hotel, joined me, worried.

"What time is dinner tonight?"

"Nine o'clock."

"Do I have time to get some sleep before getting ready?"

"It's five o'clock, you have all the time you want. Are you sure you're up for it though? Your face is..."

"Yes yes, I'm fine, I just have to rest. I'll just go to my room, put on the burn cream and go to bed. We'll meet at the hotel bar around half past seven and I'll tell you everything, okay?"

"What do you mean 'everything'? Whose sweater is that?"

The sweater! I had forgotten to give it back to Michele, I had even forgotten that I was still wearing it. How stupid! Poor Michele, I thought, he had gone out to buy beer and found himself rescuing a stranger, paying for her cream, coffee, sandwich, water, taxi and, in the end, he had even lost his sweater.

"Earth to Anna?" Lisa urged me, not having received an answer.

"Yes, I'm sorry, something absurd happened to me today, but it would take too long to tell you. I'll do it tonight."

"Okay." She looked puzzled. "Relax."

That nap had been refreshing, I thought as I dried my hair. I had regained my strength and felt full of energy. My mind was projecting frames of the afternoon spent with Michele, each time leaving me with my breath caught halfway between my throat and stomach. I was half an hour away from meeting Lisa and I was almost ready. In any case, she would be late so I could take it easy. I looked in the mirror and, looking into my own eyes, I asked myself what had happened to me that day. I had felt very strong emotions for a man I knew nothing about. But they were real. They were uncontrollable and they were... still present.

"It would be better if you came to your senses", I told myself aloud.

At that moment I realized that I had never got around to calling Lorenzo back. Alarmed, I hurried to look for my cell phone buried in the sheets and, as soon as I found it, I started the call. Would I have been in the same rush under different circumstances? How many times had I forgot when travelling? And what about him? It often happened to him too when he was at work. Why then did I feel the urge to speak to him right away? Only one answer seemed appropriate: guilt.

The phone rang empty, normally on the third ring I would have hung up but this time I waited until the line dropped. I wrote a message.

"I'm sorry, I went back to the hotel and I fell asleep, now my back is better, soon I'm going out to dinner with Lisa but call whenever you want."

I sent it without rereading it but then I did it. The guilt was evident in my words, I had provided many details that I normally would have omitted.

Of course, because you don't normally have to disguise the fact that you have been with a man who has rocked your soul.

I was ready: dress, makeup, only my shoes were missing. I took the suitcase and opened the separate compartment where I had stored them, reaching inside for my boots, and my fingers touched something I could not identify. A card? No, it looked more like an envelope, I grabbed it with my index and middle finger and pulled it out of the suitcase. It was just an envelope, one of those that normally contain letters. The front was white but turning it I found my name written on it.

I thought I knew who wrote it and immediately got the feeling that it was something serious. I sat up in bed and, crossing my legs, took a deep breath and opened it.

Dear Anna.

First of all, I want to apologize to you for letting you find this letter at a time when, I know, you could have enjoyed yourself. I'm sorry if I'll ruin your vacation with Lisa. Know that I have been very torn but I am sure that I would not be able to tell you the following by looking at your face. I know because I've tried, for the past few days and for the past five years, but I've never been able to. I am aware of why I did not succeed and the reason is only one, heavy as a boulder: I was afraid of losing you. Now the situation is no different, I have the same fear because I know I'll take to take the risk, but I can no longer hide the truth from you. However, first I want you to know a few things.

I love you. This is the thing that above all I want you to understand and I feel the greatest need to tell you. We both know that I can't say it easily. I know I've made you miss a lot over the years by never opening up. I know you suffered, I'm sorry.

The night I told my mother we would never have children, I felt bad as I was saying it. I immediately realized that I had thrown a stone at our glass castle. I could feel your eyes on me during the rest of the dinner, but I didn't have the courage to look at you and, as usual, I preferred to hide in my inflexibility.

Later I came home and saw you asleep in the armchair in front of the lit fireplace. I put out the fire because I didn't think it was safe, but then I went out again. I understood that you fell asleep while you were waiting to talk to me and I was not ready.

Even that afternoon, when you found the strength to face me, I knew the time had come, but I hoped to be able to postpone with the excuse of my trip. You were right, it was a matter that had to be discussed urgently, but I couldn't do it.

Even that day I lied to you, at least in part I did.

Your words of that evening still ring in my head now and frighten me as they did then. You told me you would leave if you realized you were living in a marriage where you weren't valued. I felt like I was dying.

The morning I waited for you in the kitchen to have breakfast, when I was the one who addressed the subject, that was the moment I came closest. I was going to tell you but it had been too long now and I believed that there was no way I would be able to keep you with me if I was honest. But I thought back to your words and, in that moment, I knew it was right. It was right for you to have the opportunity to decide for your life, it was also right you could choose to become a mother, without me. It was painful but it was right. And then something clicked and I wanted to be a different man, a better husband, more present, more attentive. It was easy to do so and that gave me hope. But now I want to be a fair husband, because I have failed in that.

The truth I hid from you dates back to five years ago, when we moved into our home. After a few months of trying to conceive without results, I decided to get a check up. I just wanted to be careful, even the doctor who prescribed the exams told me that they were not necessary at all after only three months of trying. But the fact is, Anna, I was thinking of Carlo and Lisa and I wanted to make sure you and I didn't have to go through that ordeal. Once I made sure everything was okay, I would feel better even if it took some time. When Angelo contacted you to offer you the job and you asked me to stop trying, I had already had the results of my exam. I already knew I was sterile.

I suffered a lot and I didn't have the strength to talk about it, then anger made me react and from that moment I threw myself headfirst into work. I knew I was neglecting you but I also knew I couldn't make you happy, so slowly I became what you saw. A cold, impenetrable, emotionless man. Everything that you would not have deserved to have next to you.

As I write, I'm trying to picture you reading my words and I hate myself for not being where I should be, next to you, but as I've written, I am unable to watch you suffer and, perhaps, I am such a coward that I do not want to see the hatred you are surely feeling towards me. In this too I know I have failed.

Now fear is making me want to write you a thousand

other things, a thousand excuses, a thousand justifications, but the only thing that matters I've already written before. I love you.

Lorenzo

At the exact moment I finished reading, there was a knock on the door and I thought Lorenzo must be there. He had come to try not to lose me, not to let me go, he had come to help me get out of bed. A knock again. The thing was, I didn't want to see him, I didn't want to face him. The door opened slowly.
"Anna? Everything OK?"
As soon as I saw Lisa's head peeking out, suddenly a wave of pain swept through my chest and crashed, causing me to burst into desperate tears.
With a bolt Lisa ran up to me and hugged me. "What happened, Anna?"
Sobs prevented me from answering her, so she pressed on firmly. "Anna, you're scaring me. I can't help you if you don't tell me what's going on."
With a slow gesture I passed her the letter that I still held in my hands and which, in part, was wet with tears. She looked at me and gently asked me: "May I?"
I nodded and Lisa began to read in a low voice. With deep breaths I managed to master that crisis for a few minutes and calmed down. Waiting for Lisa to finish, I turned to look at her and saw her wide eyes and troubled expression.
My stomach tightened in a painful contraction and I suddenly got up, ran to the bathroom and knelt in front of the toilet bowl. Lisa came up behind me and pulled my hair back and held it as I let out my

anxieties.

"How are you feeling?" she finally asked, handing me a bottle of water.

"I feel nothing." I took a sip and felt my throat burn.

"I'm so sorry, Anna, I wish I could do something to make you feel better."

" I know."

"What are you going to do?"

"If I had to answer you now, the only thing would be to stay here. In Barcelona. At least until I understand with what intentions I'll return home."

"He seems really scared of losing you."

"He lied to me for five years."

"I know, there are no excuses."

"Exactly! There are no excuses. And I will never forgive him for deceiving me." I felt the anger growing inside of me.

"I wouldn't have expected it from Lorenzo."

"Oh, I would! Him? Admitting not being able to procreate? Confessing a lack of manhood? Not knowing how to fulfill one's duty towards humanity? Even the smallest of men is capable of doing it and he who is so big, so pompous, so immensely full of himself, could he ever tell his wife that he is not up to this task?"

"You're saying horrible things." Lisa was looking at me with a serious expression and seemed hurt. But I was in a rage.

"That's not what I think. Of course not. It is his view of the world. For him, that's how things are."

"You can't know for sure."

"What are you doing? Are you defending him? Are you on my side every now and then or am I always in the wrong for you?"

Lisa didn't answer. With a deep breath I sent that wave of anger back. "Forgive me, I'm out of my mind."

"I understand."

"Yes, but I don't want to take it out on you, on the contrary, thanks for being here, I don't know what I would do if you weren't." The sobs started again, first slowly and then louder and louder.

"Calm down, Anna, calm down, I'm here, I'm not going anywhere."

"I am... I am... a... monster."

"Why are you saying this?"

"You are here... with me... and I... I have offended you."

"You didn't offend me." She stroked my forehead. "Our friendship is not that weak." This last sentence made me abandon even the last strengths with which I was trying to control the crying and finally I gave up, letting everything out. I cried for an indefinite amount of time and when, finally, I felt I had nothing left inside of me, I was empty. Exhausted. I wanted to fall asleep and wake up two days later.

"Damn, it's half past eight!" Lisa exclaimed suddenly looking at the watch on her wrist.

"We have to go," I whispered, my breath still broken by the long cry.

"Are you feeling up for it though?"

"No."

"Okay, then let me call and let them know."

"It doesn't seem right. Let's go, come on."

"Don't worry, If I were in your shoes, I wouldn't want to go either." After canceling dinner, Lisa came up to me again, embracing me. "Would you like to eat something?"

"Not really, but I think I need it"

"All right, honey, I'll take care of you tonight."

Later Lisa ordered burgers - meat for her and vegetarian for me - fries and ice cream.

"A perfect mix to keep our spirits up," she said.

"And our cholesterol", I added.

She went to her room to make herself comfortable and I laid out on the bed with the Tiffany blue bedspread as a tablecloth. As she arranged the sheets, the letter emerged and I found myself holding it in my hands again. With no intention of reopening it, I nervously tossed it into my bag.

Lisa returned, carrying her work computer.

"Wacky, comedy or action?" she asked me.

"Is it possible to have all three together?" I replied with my mouth full.

"I got it!" And started Ocean's Eleven.

"That's not wacky."

"It's fun and the cast is begging to be looked at."

"That's true... excellent choice."

I fell asleep somewhere in the middle of the movie, and when it was over, I heard Lisa closing the computer, putting away the boxes of food, and taking something out of the closet. I kept my eyes closed so as not to definitively abandon that state of semi-sleep. Lisa covered me and then approached me giving me a motherly kiss on the forehead. I imagined that she did the same with Pietro before putting him to sleep. Then I heard her crawl into bed and thought she really was the best friend one could have.

12

The light coming from the window looked like an incandescent blade and I kept my eyes half closed so as not to let the glow in all at once. I turned and saw that Lisa was no longer in bed, I called for her and not getting an answer I realized that she was not even in the room.

I sat up leaning against the white faux leather backrest. I felt a slight discomfort in my back but I realized that the burn had improved a lot. I remained in that position looking around the room.

On the white walls there were paintings depicting leaves whose frames matched the color of the bedspread, a vase on the desk at the foot of the bed contained a bunch of sand-colored Pampas grass. I thought my red suitcase leaning against the wall didn't quite match the decor. It was all pastel tones with the exception of the floor, which was almost black. I turned to look behind me at the picture above the bed that dominated the room. It was the only one with a framed image of the city: the colorful buildings of Parque Guell glittered in the sunrays and contrasted the blue of the sky. I thought I would like to go there before I went home.

Yes... because I would have to come back soon, the idea of staying in Barcelona until I cleared my mind no longer seemed to make sense that morning.

I let the thought return to the letter, that cursed letter I had been dreaming of all night and which now, in the light of a new day, didn't seem less serious. Not even a little.

What would I have said to Lorenzo once I crossed the threshold of the house?

If I tried to put my anger for him lying aside, I still couldn't see the situation with less hostility. Of course, it was not his will to not be able to have children but, despite this being clear to me, I just couldn't feel feelings of compassion for the man who had not let me in on something that, obviously, also concerned me.

"It is fair you could choose to become a mother, without me". Those words rang in my mind like the tune of a catchy song.

Of course that's right! Did you only notice it now? And then I wondered how I would have taken it if he had told me then, five years ago, when he had found out. What would I have done?

Would I have left him as he had feared? *Of course not! I'm not that kind of woman.*

But would I have accepted it? I could not find an answer, but undoubtedly we could have thought of alternatives. Adoption, for example. However, that was not the point, not the only one. Lying to me for all that time, Lorenzo had thrown a much more important question in my face: mutual trust and respect. For fear of losing me he had kept me in the dark, effectively depriving me of the possibility of deciding. He must have been very unsure of our love. What if over time I had really put aside the idea of becoming a mother? Wouldn't he have ever told me? Would we have lived together *"until death did us part"* with that secret nestled in the ice of his heart? Heart, what heart? A man capable of doing such a thing could not have a heart!

It is the pride that pulse in his veins, just that.

I realized that I was still deeply angry. Last night had not healed the wound.

Lisa reappeared in the room. "Ah good, you're awake! Good morning, sleeping beauty."

"Good morning to you too, how late is it?"

"It's a quarter past ten."

"Wow, I slept a lot, have you been up for a long time?" I asked noticing that she was still wearing her pajamas.

"I wouldn't say that, I woke up just in time to run down for breakfast. Cream or jam?" She handed me the basket with the croissants that gave off an inviting scent.

"Great, breakfast in bed! Is there coffee too?" I took the jam croissant knowing I was doing her a favor.

"Obviously." She sat down next to me. "How are you feeling today? Did the night bring any precious advice?"

"The night didn't even take the anger away. And that's how I feel... mad."

"Come on, get dressed", she said after finishing the coffee, "we're going to be tourists today."

"I don't know if I can," I replied, smiling.

"You will. Put on the best dress you have in your

suitcase, fix yourself up and I'll come pick you up in half an hour and take you to lunch."

"Should I put on heels?"

"Sure."

"But then we'll be uncomfortable walking in heels all day."

"Nobody talked about walking. As I said, today we are tourists." And then she added, winking: "VIPs"

"Okay", I replied without too much enthusiasm, "I trust you."

Ready to go out, I grabbed my bag from the chair and saw Michele's sweater resting there. I lingered for a moment then I took it in my hands, when I buried my face inside to breathe its scent, I still felt the tightness in my stomach I had felt the previous afternoon. Uncontrolled flashes of his face had appeared to me without interruption that morning, during the night and, I had to admit, even the evening before. Despite what happened, my mind had continued its projection. I remember that on a couple of occasions I had pushed my thoughts back almost in anger, as if the figure that crept into my head was violating a space that was too personal.

But in that moment, the scent of his sweater put a smile on my face again, and seeing his in my memories was nice, exciting.

Outside the hotel I waited for Lisa to call a taxi, but instead she walked away inviting me to follow her.

"Didn't we say no walking?"

"It's nine minutes on foot, do you think you can do it? Ten years ago we would have traveled three times the distance in heels double the height."

"Ten years ago we wore heels every weekend", I laughed, thinking back to those good old days.

"I like the dress, is it new?"

I had put the floral one on and now that I was wearing it, I was glad I chose it, I liked it too. Truthfully, the heels weren't that high and, although I wasn't used to wearing them anymore, walking wasn't painful.

"Where are we going?"

"There's a place close by someone recommended, it seems very nice and it's by the sea."

"Who recommended it to you?"

"My client and his friend."

"Oh yeah, right, we blew them up last night. How did they take it?"

"I told them you weren't feeling well."

"They must have believed it," I said sarcastically.

"Who cares," Lisa said.

"I'm sorry though, they were nice to invite us."

"If you want, I can call them and ask them to join us for lunch."

I spent a few seconds imagining lunch with Lisa, not that I didn't want to spend it with her, but I had the unpleasant feeling that we would go back to the "letter" topic again and I didn't feel like it.

"Yes, come on, try, at least out of politeness."

Lisa made the call but to no avail, then left a message.

It was a sunny day, the sky clear and the weather pleasant. Sitting at the One Ocean Club table, we were enjoying the view over Port Vell crowded with private boats and small yachts. The place was very elegant and we had filled out a form for "non-members" before taking our seats. The staff were friendly and helpful and we had every intention of being spoiled. There was also a wine expert who recommended the right pairing for each course. *A real treat*, I thought. I had no intention of spoiling that moment with negative thoughts and when, looking for the handkerchief in my purse, the letter fell into my hand, I pushed it aside without giving it any importance. Apparently.

Lisa saw that movement and looked at me suspiciously. "Listen, you didn't tell me about the absurd thing that happened to you yesterday... so, whose sweater was it?"

I smiled with an ironically guilty look. "You can't even imagine, I passed out in a man's arms."

Lisa was drinking a strawberry cocktail which she chocked on causing her to cough a little. "Come on, talk," she said, her eyes wide with curiosity.

I told her what had happened in great detail, I told her that when I turned to the man I had started to stutter in the throes of a tornado of emotions that had not subsided for much of the time we had spent together. Until I passed out. I told her that I had fallen asleep on his shoulder as he took a ride back to the hotel with me and that when I woke up I felt embarrassed and guilty. I explained that I could not control those feelings but that at a certain point I had felt the urge to leave. As if I sensed a danger in continuing that meeting. My friend looked at me with an amazed, curious and incredulous expression.

"What was he like?" she asked me.

"As I told you he was fascinating, he must have been more or less our age. He wore a white polo shirt and faded jeans. I was also struck by his peaceful and relaxed attitude. He seemed to be at peace with the whole world. He was persuasive."

"It seems to me he persuaded you." She laughed, and I with her.

"Let's not get out of line, I was still under the effect of the sun" I pointed out trying to find some decency within myself.

"Do you think that was the cause of the fainting?"

"The sunburn? Yes... Besides, I hadn't eaten anything."

"What about the sweater? How did it end up on you?"

"Stop being mischievous! He lent me the sweater because I was shivering from the cold. I just didn't realize I was still wearing it when we split up."

"He will have noticed by now," replied the lawyer.

"He might have done it out to be polite."

"He might have done it to see you again." It made me think about Michele's last offer: *"If we meet again, you will offer me a drink."*

For a moment I thought that Lisa's reasoning might make sense.

"No, he wouldn't know how to contact me", I replied, denying that possibility, especially to myself.

" Well, he knows where you are staying."

"It makes no difference, I have other things to think about," I said looking at the bag out of the corner of my eye. Then I tried to change the subject. "Did the client answer you?"

"Let me check." Lisa took the phone from her purse. "Yes, he says they're nearby and will join us here."

Good, better distract ourselves from this memory too.

"Look, Anna..." When my friend started a sentence that way, I knew she would tell me something serious.

"Yes."

"Last night I considered something about Lorenzo's letter."

Here we go. I took a breath and listened.

"Shoot."

"I don't know, it's just an idea that came to me, but don't you think it's strange that he got check ups for such a short time?"

"Well," I said, picturing my husband making that decision. "No, knowing him, it doesn't surprise me that much."

"I know, but you see... from experience I know that men..."

"Counsel." A male voice interrupted Lisa who stood up. I followed her and stood up as well.

"Well, good morning. This is Anna."

"Nice to meet you, Anna, how are you feeling today?"

"Much better, thanks, in fact I apologize for last night. Pleased to meet you." Squeezing his hand, I watched him. He was very different from how I pictured him, and although he was a nice-looking man, I was expecting someone particularly handsome from Lisa's description.

"Miguel, right?"

"No, sorry, I'm Alex." *Alex who?* A moment of confusion.

"Were you just around the corner?" Lisa asked.

"My buddy woke up a romantic this morning, we crossed the city because he wanted to walk on the beach."

"Ah, and where is he?"

"He was on the phone, he'll be... ah, there he is over there."

Suddenly the world around me stopped, no movement, no noise, I could only hear the pattern of my breathing in my ears. Could it be him? No, impossible, my mind is playing a trick on me, I thought. It would have been too absurd a coincidence. After all, coincidences always seem so, don't they? Yet, as he got closer to us, the uncertainty left me and the excitement grew.

"Lisa, didn't you tell me your client was Spanish?" I whispered to her without taking my eyes off the man.

"No no, he's Italian, his name is Miguel but he's from Perugia."

I focused. It was him.

He walked at a leisurely pace, but suddenly, looking at me, he stopped walking. He stood still for a few seconds as if stunned and it was then that Alex called him.

"Miky?! Have you seen a ghost?"

He started walking again and joined us. "Counsel", he said, addressing Lisa with a nod that resembled a slight bow.

"Anna, happy to see you again."

A not too spontaneous smile was all I offered as a reply.

We sat around the table. On my right Lisa alternately looked at Michele - or Miguel - first and then at me without stopping, on the left Alex did the same. Michele, on the other hand, seemed uninterested in explaining and kept his gaze fixed on me making my blood boil. I thought I saw a faint smile of satisfaction on his lips.

"So it's my turn to pay for a drink, right... Miguel?" I emphasized the name provocatively and he smiled and nodded.

It all seemed absurd, so absurd that I even got the idea that he already knew we would see each other again. Maybe that was why he had invited Lisa and me to dinner the night before. No, it was impossible, the invitation was prior to our meeting.

"I don't understand", I protested suddenly, "if Lisa was busy with the auction, why were you downtown with me yesterday?"

At that point Lisa understood that "her" Miguel was the same man I had told her about earlier. The owner of the sweater. And I saw her smile amused by the gag.

"Lisa stayed to take care of some paperwork and my presence was unnecessary."

"Wait a minute..." Alex interrupted him, reaching out towards his friend. "You mean to tell me that yesterday, while I waited two hours at the hotel for you to come back with the beers, you were with her?"

Michele laughed. "Yes, but it was an emergency."

Alex turned to look at me and then back to Michele. "I can imagine. Thanks, Anna, the hot beers were delicious."

"I'm sorry." I laughed.

We ordered fish, the wine was recommended to us by the sommelier and the choice seemed right. Lunch was entertaining and fun, only when our eyes met did I feel a strange discomfort. Lisa seemed to clearly spot that hidden and involuntary game between me and Michele, every now and then I felt her foot kicking my leg under the table. When it came time for coffee we all seemed at ease, enjoying each other's pleasant company. A cheerful but excessively loud ringtone caught our attention and we looked around trying to locate the owner of the phone.

"It's yours," Michele said to his friend.

"Oh, that's right, I changed my ringtone and I can never recognize it." Looking at the screen he added: "It's Federica."

That seemed to worry him and he looked at Michele who dismissed him with a wave, as if to say: *she called you, you deal with it.*

"Oh yeah? Then I'll put it on speakerphone."

"Hello."

"Hola!" a shrill voice answered. "I was just calling to make sure you're enjoying yourselves." She paused, then added emphasizing the words: "Without me."

"Come on, Fede, piss off, you know we came for another reason", Alex chuckled.

"Yeah, yeah, sure, right! By the way, how did the business go?"

"Great," said Michele. "The house is mine!"

"Ahhh, you're there too! Yayyy, I'm happy for you! Next time you go back to Barcelona you have to take me with you though."

"Of course."

They spoke with the familiarity of people who have known each other for a long time.

"Anyway..." continued the girl on the phone, "I know very well that you used the excuse of the house to go to Barcelona to celebrate the bachelor party! And I will never forgive you for it!"

"What are you even saying, Fede! It wouldn't be fun without you." The two friends giggled without being heard.

"Come on, I promise you we'll celebrate together next weekend."

"Yes, and in the meantime you got the *dude stuff* out of the way there! Nice plan."

The girl seemed amused, even if she pretended to be offended. "Anyway, Miky, when you come back promise to fill me in on how Al behaved, and you'll have to tell me everything!"

"Sorry, why Al? Why do you want to only know about me?"

"Who else? His Holiness, Father Michele? I can't even imagine!"

At that sentence Lisa and I burst out laughing and

Michele, apparently embarrassed, decided to cut the phone call short. "Thanks, I'd say you've ruined my reputation enough for today. We'll talk soon."

"No, wait. What reputation? Who are you with?" Alex, his friend's accomplice, ended the call while the girl's voice could still be heard.

"Is there a wedding in sight, then?" Lisa asked, looking at Alex who sat opposite her.

"Don't look at me", he said, raising his hands. "Been there, done that, and already paid! He's the crazy one this time." He nodded his head toward Michele.

Here it was, news that I really did not expect. Michele was engaged. Although I expected to feel some repulsion about it, I actually had no reactions, neither internal nor external. Of course, it had surprised me, and I couldn't deny that I felt a veil of annoyance, when he later admitted that he was close to walking down the altar, however, all in all, I was reassured by my almost indifference to that discovery.

"When's the wedding?" I asked Michele looking him straight in the eye without any hesitation. I was proud of myself, the spell was broken.

It was just the sunburn.

" 'Funny guy' here, is getting married in August. To the delight of us guests who, in addition to dying of heat, will also have to interrupt our holidays!" Alex intervened.

"Not cool," Lisa confirmed as she sipped the wine.

"I didn't have a choice, that's my only free time and the one month Mery can take time off work too."

"And how long have you and Mery known each other?" continued my friend, who seemed more interested in the details of that wedding than I was.

"Since university. We were classmates and we graduated together. Practically a lifetime." While speaking Michele drew imaginary lines on the white tablecloth with his knife. And then, turning to Lisa who had now become his only counterpart, he asked her: "How about you?"

"I have been married for twelve years and have a seven year old boy."

"How wonderful! What's his name?"

"His name is Pietro."

"He's adorable," I smiled at my friend.

"And you, Anna, how long have you been married?" It was Michele this time who turned to me, looking me straight in the eye, though I caught something in his expression that looked like a mixture of defiance and revenge. I found it annoying, but maybe it was just my impression.

"Nine years."

He pointed and nodded at my left hand resting on the table. "I didn't notice it yesterday, did you have it?"

"What? Her ring?" Lisa intervened. "In the last nine years I've never seen that finger without a ring, she doesn't even take it off to take a shower."

I smiled, admitting it was true.

"No children?" he asked again, touching a sore spot unknowingly.

"No children." I lowered my eyes and, considering his silence, I assumed that he understood that he had hit a nerve.

"I have been married for seven years and separated for two, a five year old daughter who is the most beautiful thing in the world. I say that in case someone is interested, I'm starting to feel left out." Alex caused yet another laugh.

Separated with a very young girl. I thought it was very sad and I wondered with what logic, at times,

God's plans were made.

"How come no children, Anna?" Alex shot that arrow straight into my chest. Michele approached his friend suggesting that the question was not very delicate and he apologized.

"We can't have any," I declared. I did it more to tell myself than to inform them. For the first time I put myself in those new shoes, for the first time I had an answer to give to that question. It was a strange sensation, and when Michele placed his hand on mine, I found comfort in his gesture.

Alex apologized again then declared that it was time to change the subject.

At the end of the meal, Michele asked for the bill and I thought that, once we got up from the table, we would never see each other again. For real this time.

I took the bag looking for my wallet and, again, Lorenzo's letter ended up in my hand. I never found anything in there, and yet that thing... it seemed it was looking for me.

At that moment, however, I grabbed it, keeping my hand hidden in the bag. Perhaps due to the events of that day, a strong wave of heat invaded my stomach and my eyes filled with tears.

Without lifting my head I passed the wallet into Lisa's hands. "Here, you pay please, pay for them too."

"Do you feel sick?"

"I just need to get out for a second."

13

"Shall we take a stroll through the center together?"

Lisa, Alex and Michele had exited the place and I was waiting for them, as cheerful as possible. The offer provoked a crossing of glances.

"I have to go and collect the keys to the house. Would you like to come with me?" Michele offered as he took his cell phone out of the back pocket of his jeans.

"A captivating proposal, friend, congratulations!"

"What a fool you are, it'll take me a minute. Anyway, if you're not up for it, I'll join you guys later."

"Excellent, do you have any preferences, ladies?"

"I'm warning you not to call us that, you can't even imagine what she did to the last man who dared doing so," I said, pointing to Lisa.

"Well said, sister."

"Listen... sister, wouldn't it be better if we went to

the hotel to change our shoes?"

"Absolutely not, it's still our VIP day, we'll call a taxi."

"I'm calling one too," said Michele, "I'll have them send two."

The first car arrived and we left it to Michele for his errand. As he was about to get in, he stopped. "I don't want to go alone though," he said with a very false childish pout.

"I'm not coming, I've been following you for this house stuff for three days and now I'll leave you to your business, dear friend."

"Come on, you're cruel! Girls?"

Was I tempted? Very much. Would I have offered? Certainly not.

"I'll take the realtor for a walk and you assist the buyer?" Lisa suggested looking me straight in the eye. I had the impression that she was studying the situation, as if she were trying to read me and, at the same time, test me to see what was going to happen.

At that point I had to make a choice, and that's what I did.

The taxi rolled slowly through the city traffic and it seemed to me it was heading north. Michele sat next to me with his eyes focusing on what was outside.

"Do you have to go to the house?" I asked breaking the silence.

"No no, I have to collect the keys from someone in charge, it wasn't possible yesterday. Thank you for coming with me."

"I was indebted."

"You paid for the drinks."

"It's true, then we're even." He laughed and I smiled too.

"We're here, it'll take me a minute."
"Should I wait for you in the taxi or let him go?"
"You decide."
I got out of the car and Michele paid the taxi driver.
While I waited for him outside the building I was looking for something familiar to understand where we were. No idea.
I only realized we were north of the city. The street was narrow and dimly lit by the sun, it looked like it was already evening in that alley. I didn't much like being there alone. I had read several articles on the Barcelona underworld and many news of pickpocketing, robberies or worse always started with a woman, preferably a foreigner, alone and lost.
I thought about the painting on the bed and I was curious to see how far Parque Guell was, but I didn't have time because Michele reappeared from the door of the decadent building and joined me, crossing the street.
"One minute exactly."
"I'm a man of my word." He jangled the keys in front of my eyes.
"Do you know how far Parque Guell is?" I asked.
"Sure, it's back here, do you want to go?"
"I would like to, but we have to join the other two."

Michele took the phone out of his pocket, he certainly did not let himself be influenced by negative thoughts like me, plus he seemed to know the city very well. "My phone's dead. Can I call Alex with yours?"
"Sure, I don't have his number though."
"No need, I know it by heart."

As I handed him the phone, his hand touched mine.

My heart trembled.

"Al, it's Miky, would you like to join us at Guell?" There was a brief silence. "Perfect, we'll be waiting for you there." He ended the call and handed the phone back to me.

"As always, you have a solution for everything."

"Other wishes, milady?"

"Not at the moment, thanks."

I watched him move naturally through the streets of that city as if he had always been used to living there. He was as charming as I remembered him, breathing in the scent of his sweater.

Beside him I felt protected, guided, I had the impression that he would solve every problem we encountered and I could enjoy those moments without thinking about anything.

We got on a bus which, after three stops, dropped us off at the park entrance. The steps at the entrance dominated the scene, they were impressive and elegant. We walked around making small talk: the weather, the people, the traffic of the city. I realized that we shared a note of embarrassment and he too, who had always seemed calm and at ease to me, now seemed less genuine.

On the Carrube overpass the sun filtered through the columns, lighting up the stones that seemed incandescent. The day was mild, it wasn't as hot as my afternoon on the beach, but it was fine without a jacket.

When we got to the highest part of the park we crossed the square to reach the panoramic wall from which you can admire the deep blue of the sea, as well as the whole city. I recognized the buildings in the photo and felt satisfaction in being there.

The kaleidoscope of colors on the walls was enhanced by the sun illuminating it, just like in the painting, and we agreed that Gaudi's works were wonderful. Lively and elegant at the same time. The sun warmed the skin pleasantly, and the same heat also melted the bit of the cold that kept us distant.

"I can't believe I saw you again this way" he exclaimed, shaking his head.

"Yes, it's absurd. I really had to pay for that drink," I said in a falsely annoyed tone.

"I enjoyed chatting with you yesterday."

"You must have Prince Charming Syndrome, then."

"Which is?"

"The young man who saves the damsel in distress."

He laughed. "Maybe, but you don't strike me as a damsel who likes to be saved by others." His shoulder playfully hit mine.

"I see you got me all figured out... in such a short time too."

Little by little he was getting closer and closer to my private sphere, it was strange how it didn't bother me. I had the feeling that we had known each other forever.

"Can I ask you something very personal?" he asked at that point, turning his face towards me.

I looked at him and I found him even more beautiful than before, he was sitting with one leg dangling and the other folded on the wall, he had a neat but not too elegant look, he wore a white shirt, perhaps linen, with the sleeves rolled up to his elbows and a pair of black jeans. I thought he looked great dressed like that.

"You can try", I replied, not too convinced.

"I'd like to know what happened to you today, when you left the restaurant with tears in your eyes."

"How did you spot the tears?"

"I don't know."

"A feeling maybe?" I asked making fun of him.

I glanced over my shoulder, the roofs spread like a carpet leading down to the sea. How could I explain it? Where to start? I took the bag.

Michele followed my movements, he seemed curious. I looked for it, sure I wasn't going to miss it and pulled out the letter. I handed it to him and he looked at me hesitantly, undecided whether to take it or not.

"Read this."

"What is it?"

"Lorenzo is my husband," I just replied and watched him as he opened the envelope and then as he read the letter. Though his expression was impenetrable, there was a moment when he took my hand and I knew he had got to a painful part. He kept his gaze fixed on Lorenzo's words while his hand clasped mine.

At one point he looked up at me and stood still, as if he were digesting the words he had read. His dark eyes were so intense that I got the impression they were painting mine black too.

Only after a few moments did he speak to me: "You didn't know anything?"

"Nothing."

"And did you find out like that? From this letter?"

I nodded.

Michele shook his head. "When did you read it?"

"Last night."

"Now I understand."

"What?"

"Why you were feeling bad."

I ventured a half smile, then we stood in silence staring at the blue sky for a few minutes, hand in hand. I didn't understand what the reason was, but I felt I was exactly where I wanted to be.

"Did you cry?" he asked.

"A lot," I replied.

"Because of his lie?"

"I think so, it was a cry of rage."

"And now? What are you going to do?"

"I have no idea. I think I'll just indulge the feelings that will emerge when I see him again."

With his fingers he touched the gold wedding ring I had on my ring finger and moved it around. "Didn't that make you want to take off your ring either?"

I shook my head. "It would take more than that."

"What?"

"Divorce."

14

In the taxi that took us back to the hotel, Lisa wanted to know everything in detail. I told her that I had made Michele read the letter, according to her it was the right move.

"You needed an outside opinion, someone who could give a detached judgment." I thought that was not the reason that had prompted me to do it, but I agreed with her all the same. Back at the hotel I checked the phone, there was a message from Angelo. In all that commotion, I hadn't thought about work anymore.

"*Hi Anna, I hope you are well, I would like to ask you if you can come to the newsroom next week.*"

I dialed the number and called him.

"Anna... hi." Judging from his tone, he sounded embarrassed.

"Hi, I've read the message. Is everything okay?"

"I'd rather talk about it in person."

Since I already knew what it was, I insisted on having him confess. "Okay but... did something happen?"

"Yup."

"Something bad?"

"I'd like to see you, because there are many things to say and... well, it could be both bad and good. I don't want to tell you anything else."

Those words surprised me, but I realized that my mind was not ready to welcome more news. "Monday at nine ok?" I just asked him.

"Yes, see you on Monday."

Before then, I thought I knew why he was calling me, but at the end I wasn't sure anymore. *Both bad and good*, he'd said. I was curious, but I knew I couldn't speed up the time.

At dinner I didn't want the conversation to fall back to Lorenzo, but the subject was pending and I felt the need to know what followed, so I confronted Lisa as soon as we sat down at the table. "What did you want to tell me today, when Alex interrupted us?"

"Forget it, it wasn't anything important."

"I'd like to know, if you don't mind, I got the impression that you understood something that escapes me."

"All right," she said, settling into her chair, "but please take it for what it is: just an idea." She put down her fork and devoted herself carefully to what she meant. She seemed to be looking for the right words.

"As I was telling you today, during our ordeal Carlo and I met many couples who, like us, had difficulty conceiving and I swear to you that each of those men hated to undergo a spermiogram. Including Carlo. And then I wondered why Lorenzo, on the other hand, did it of his own free will without, among other things, a valid motivation at that moment. It's like..."

"Like he already suspected it." My thoughts followed the logical thread of that speech and I finished the sentence Lisa didn't seem to want to.

"Exactly."

"And how can I find out?"

"I don't know, I think at this point only he can tell you."

"Who? Mister Sincerity?" I replied annoyed by the feeling of anger that Lorenzo's lie caused me. "How could he have suspected it?"

"I don't know, but I remember that some of the sterile people we met knew they could be, some from cancer, some from a virus, some from surgery."

I concentrated on thinking about what problems my husband might have had, but I couldn't remember any of them. I didn't even think he'd ever gotten sick in those fourteen years.

"Well, I can't come up with anything, anyway I'll think it over."

"Yes, but don't drive yourself crazy over this, you already have enough things to process."

I smiled at her and she took the menu, but then put it back down and turned back to me. "Listen..." she started again, "since we're already talking about it, can I ask you a question about you and Lorenzo?"

I wanted to say no, but something else came out of my mouth: "Of course."

"Before all this, do you think you were ready to have a baby?"

"Well, yes. We have been waiting for the right moment for years. By now, yes, we were there."

«No, Anna, forget the right moment, that's bullshit. If your interpret that as economic, housing, employment, mental stability... you know, when you feel you have had enough fun... no, that's bullshit. The baby arrives and all your mental fabrications about the right moment go to shit. I want to know if you and Lorenzo were ready to become parents. You and him as a couple. "

Sometimes when Lisa spoke to me with that bluntness, I felt like I was under scrutiny, afraid of saying the wrong thing. I took a breath and, trying to be casual, replied, "Well, I do, but I can only answer for myself."

"And that's already wrong."

"What do you mean? I wanted a baby... I really did."

"A baby takes a couple and turns it upside down. I'm not saying it destroys it, but anyone who has a child to keep a relationship together, really has no clue how wrong that is." She stared at me as if she wanted to find the truth in my eyes.

"Do you think that's us?" I took the bottle and filled both glasses with water.

"I certainly can't know. But I know that a couple must be strong. There must be love, yes, but also mutual respect, respect for the other's time, dedication and lots of patience." Lisa paused to look for my gaze and then went on: "It's not enough that you both want it, you have to be a team. Understanding when the other can't take it anymore and sacrificing your time to help each other not to collapse. When Pietro was one years old and I needed to go back to my life, to my job, Carlo had to rethink his commitments. You have to compensate without blaming the other for the time you are dedicating to the family. It seems obvious but it isn't. "

I lowered my eyes. "Well, on this subject I've always

imagined myself alone with the child and Lorenzo appearing in the evening for dinner and disappearing in the morning to go to work."

"Sure, this happens, especially in the beginning, but it's not that easy, you know? When you spend all day dedicating yourself to your child, at home, when they sleep and instead of resting you look around and start doing chores. In the evening, when your husband gets home, sometimes you want to throw your child at him and run away. There are not many mothers who admit it, because with a newborn, a sense of guilt also arises. It is an exhausting feeling that makes you question all certainties and makes you feel wrong in wanting something for yourself. There, in that case, you need a man who understands that, who will look at you and tell you you're doing a great job, who will tell you to take a moment for yourself because you deserve it. And he has to tell you, that you deserve it, because in that whirlwind of emotions, struggle and sacrifices, even if you can see that you're killing yourself with fatigue you don't know it, you don't feel deserving of something because your sense of responsibility is telling you that you're not doing anything but your job. "

I felt disoriented. "Why are you telling me all this?"

Without answering my question, she went on: "Another important thing is that the couple is firm in their values, in the way they face life. Raising a child also means educating them according to what you think is right. Leaving them free to become what they believe or believing you know what they should become. Do you understand what I mean?"

"Maybe."

"I say this because, from what you're telling me,

it seems you and Lorenzo never talk about you as a couple, your dreams, your projects. Everyone takes their own path fighting their own battles, never sharing them with the other. With a child this cannot be done."

Lisa's words hit me in the stomach. Her interpretation was more real than I wanted to admit.

"In any case, the problem no longer exists", I said bitterly, shrugging my shoulders. I realized, however, what I was doing so to shift the attention to Lorenzo's lie, to his "guilt", in order to hide all the shortcomings we had as a couple.

"It exists alright" she insisted while deboning the fish on her plate.

"What do you mean?"

"I mean now you have the opportunity to ask yourself if your desire for motherhood depends on the need to fill a void, or on the desire to create a life."

Lying on the bed I stared at the ceiling leaving my mind free to wander uncontrolled. I was exhausted, but too many questions and too many emotions kept me from falling asleep. I was thinking of Lorenzo, of the secret he had kept for five years, or who knows how long, if Lisa was right. I thought about our marriage and how many times I had wondered if it was right the way it was. Our never speaking, the way we guided our lives individually by sharing little and nothing. Sometimes I felt like I was only living while on the road. What would my life have been like without that essential part? A child would have taken it from me, at least for a while. I had always thought that having a creature to take care of, to raise and love, I wouldn't feel the weight of that sacrifice, but now I wondered if it wasn't actually a desire to fill a void in that part of my life. It was a horrible thought that already made me feel unworthy to become a mother. But perhaps I must have had a little maternal instinct, if I already harbored a sense of guilt for a creature that wasn't there yet. And that would never come.

And then again questions in my head. How would I have addressed the subject with Lorenzo? How would he have reacted? Weren't we ready for a child? Back then, would his infertility have saved our marriage? I refused to accept that idea.

He had called me back the evening of the letter, but I had already found it and had not wanted to speak to him. I still didn't want to and for this reason I hadn't tried to reach him. I was thinking of Michele and I hated myself for that. Why think of another man in the middle of all that mess? Yet I suffered at the idea that I would not see him again. At that moment I wanted to have his phone number. I didn't know if I was going to call him, but it would be less difficult to know I could do it… sooner or later. I couldn't explain how that man conquered me every second I was next to him, with a gesture, an expression, a smile. His smile.

I looked at the chair in front of me looking for his sweater, I wanted to wear it again, sleep in it, breathe its scent. But it would have been worse, it would have been torture. I felt stupid. Me, married for nine years, lying there thinking about a man who would get married in a few months. *Enough, Anna!* I told myself aloud. *This is madness.* However, I couldn't help but wonder where he was at that moment. Maybe out celebrating his bachelor party. The thought made me feel even more stupid. I wanted to stop wondering about Michele, about Lorenzo. Quit altogether, shut it down. But there was no chance I would fall asleep, I didn't even want to read and so I decided to go for a hot bath. *To relax*, I told myself.

    Immersed in the tub I felt better, put my headphones on and listened to the loud music. Coming out of the bathroom wearing a bathrobe and wet hair tied up in an impromptu turban, I saw a note sticking out from under the bedroom door. I picked it up and opened it. I only found two words written on it: *"Goodnight, Anna"*.

15

"Are you sure he's the one who left it?"

"Who else? If it wasn't you, I can't think of anyone else. "

"Yes, sure, you're right. But it is strange. How did he know your room number?"

"I have no idea."

"Plus, did he come all the way to your door just to leave you a note?"

"Apparently…"

Lisa smiled and reread the words on the piece of paper. "But it's romantic."

"Yes yes, it's romantic, but what am I supposed to do now?"

"What would you want to do?"

I didn't know how to answer.

I took the cup of coffee and breathed in its scent, the feeling of warmth of the ceramic in my hands comforted me. The hotel's breakfast room was still semi-deserted and the few people present were all standing at the buffet table. On Sunday mornings people sleep, but I had woken up before sunrise, I could hardly wait for a decent time to drag my friend to breakfast.

"What the hell do you want?" Those were her words answering the phone at seven.

"I have to talk to you, shall we go down to eat something?"

And, the true friend she is, her response was: "This friendship is killing me, I'm coming."

I thought of the sweater placed on the bed in my room, in the end I had worn it to sleep. I could have brought it to him, after all I certainly couldn't pack it and I was sorry to leave it there. Maybe it was just an excuse. Or maybe not.

"Do you want me to give you his number? I don't know, to thank him, maybe."

It's true! Lisa had his phone number. I could have called him, but to tell him what? *"Thanks for the note?" "Why didn't you knock on the door?"*

God, maybe he had! I was in the bathroom with music in my ears and I would not have been able to hear it. Maybe he wanted to see me, talk to me, maybe he had come for that reason but when he didn't get an answer he left the note. I felt a sense of frustration growing at the idea of having missed that opportunity.

In any case it was gone by now, I could not have recovered it; if I had been given an opportunity, I had missed it. Maybe it was destiny that it would go like this, after all nothing could have happened other than what we had already experienced together. Certainly neither of us could in any way indulge in a feeling that, although powerful, was definitely, deeply wrong.

"Enough, I don't want to think about it anymore,

what's the use?"

Lisa seemed surprised at my position but humored me, albeit with an unconvinced expression.

She suggested we relax on the beach that morning, check out was at ten and the reception girl kindly agreed to let us leave our bags in storage so that we could enjoy our last day in Barcelona. Our flight was scheduled for 10pm, and a car, booked by the law firm, would come pick us up at 8pm. I was in the kind of state of mind in which everything was going to be fine unless I was left alone, so, as long as I found a shady space to avoid new sunburns, I agreed. Before going up I had jumped outside to test the weather, it was still cool considering the time, but it looked like it was going to be another nice sunny day.

"Put SPF on!" Lisa had instructed me before going up to her room.

The suitcase was ready, and so was I. I checked that I hadn't forgotten anything by doing a classic room inspection. I lifted the covers to check under the bed, behind the curtains, under the desk, inside the closet and, even if I had never opened them, I looked in all the drawers.

I had everything, the only object I was deliberately forgetting was Michele's sweater. For a moment I was tempted to throw it in the suitcase, but then I thought better of it. It was better that he stayed there, along with his memory. I was on the threshold, turned towards the room for a last glance and seeing him there, abandoned on the chair, made me infinitely sad. I went back inside and took it, I would have left it at the reception, then Lisa would have sent a message to Michele saying that he could come and get it back. *Yes, good idea.*

Lisa showed up, fashionably late.

"Have you already stored your luggage?" she asked standing in front of me with a colorful sundress through which you could see her swimsuit. I hadn't brought anything like that and was wearing a pair of denim shorts and a white T-shirt.

"No, I waited for you."

The girl who worked at the reception took us to a small room which could only be accessed by passing behind the counter. After arranging our bags, she locked it. I was holding the sweater in my hand and was ready to hand it over, explaining that, perhaps, the owner would come pick it up that same day. Lisa grabbed my arm, I looked at her and she nodded towards the front door.

Seeing Michele approach us was a shot through the heart, and I felt my pulse speed up again, just like the first time, like every time he appeared unexpectedly in front of me. He stopped in the middle of the hall, smiled at me, waved to me and Lisa and then stood waiting for us. I looked at my friend: she also seemed to wonder what he had come here for. I apologized to the girl, telling her the problem was solved and headed towards Michele.

"Was she paying well for it?"

"For what?"

"My sweater. Were you selling it to her?" he asked, amused, grabbing it.

"No, I wanted to leave it here then Lisa was going to write you a text... But you came, so problem solved."

"That's kind of you, but that's not what I came for."

"Hi Michele!" Lisa said joining us.

"Good morning Lisa, listen, I have a huge favor to ask you." At the thought that he wasn't there for me, my body, which used to be as stiff as a board, relaxed and I breathed.

"Of me? Tell me, if I can help you, I'll gladly do it."

"I'd like to take Anna away from you for a very short time."

In a single contraction, every muscle of mine tightened and my breath caught in the pit of my stomach again.

"Um... yes, no problem. If she agrees."

"What do you think, Anna? Can I kidnap you?"

"Actually... I... I don't know, I don't feel like leaving Lisa alone."

"We won't be gone for long, I promise." With his right palm resting on his heart he swore again.

"Don't worry about me, I'll wait for you on the beach. Go." Lisa gave me a sincere smile that I felt I could trust.

"Where do you want to go?" I asked, turning my gaze to Michele.

"You'll see", he replied.

We left the hotel and got into the taxi that was waiting for us a few meters away.

About fifteen minutes later the car dropped us off at a large intersection. The journey was silent and the embarrassment dense inside the vehicle. I had looked at the clock mechanically almost every minute and had not mentioned the note under the door. Nothing had been said at all, to tell the truth, and those few times when our eyes met, we tried to mask the tension by smiling.

"Do you know where we are?" Michele asked me when the taxi left.

"I'm not sure."

Looking around I found the place not entirely unknown, but I could not identify it all the same.

Michele took my hand and we crossed the street, that gesture had become less extraordinary since it wasn't the first time, yet it was pure emotion again. I observed that place trying to recognize something: a detail, a building, whatever made me understand where I was. Then, looking up, I saw the plaque on the wall of the first building on the street, *"Rambla de Catalunya"*. Of course! I had been there before. That time, however, the street was a real open-air art gallery and had a completely different aspect. I remembered that there were paintings, sculptures and picture stalls on either side of the sidewalk and at every step the bright and vibrant colors of the works drew attention making it impossible to decide where to look. Now, instead, it looked calm, enveloped in the intense mid-morning light. It was still slow paced, as if waking up with baby steps, with the a kind of Sunday morning calm. I was there, a few centimeters from Michele, walking without direction. It was so absurd.

I felt the warmth of his hand, and mine seemed to have received all the blood I had in my body, it was beating as if my heart was only pumping in that direction.

Suddenly Michele stopped in front of one of the many bars that intoxicated the air with the scent of freshly baked coffee and croissants.

"Are you hungry?"

"Actually, I am", I replied, thinking that my seven-thirty breakfast had already been well digested.

"Wait here." He reappeared after a few minutes with a white bag and two brown paper cups with black lids.

"Where are we going?"

"Are you curious?"

"I'm a woman after all", I replied, uttering the first

icebreaker of the day.

"Now I'll show you, we're here."

What did he mean 'here'? All that fuss to show me Rambla de Catalunya? Yes, it was beautiful but... Plus, why get our breakfast to go when we could sit at a table on the boulevard? He asked me to hold the bag from which the scent of butter and hazelnuts came out and put his free hand in his pocket to take out a set of keys.

He opened a black door that seemed heavy, then went inside holding it open for me. I crossed the threshold, lost, I began to guess where he was taking me, but I did not understand the reason. It was cold inside and the air was humid like in a cellar. Michele walked in front of me to lead the way and, after an endless amount of high and irregular steps, we stopped in front of another door. He unlocked the door with the same keys and, with his arm stretched out, swung it open.

"After you," he said.

I entered the apartment and found myself surrounded by peeling walls and some battered furniture. The floor was intact but its ancient texture, probably dating back to the age of the building, was barely distinguishable under a layer of dust and dirt. Light barely filtered through the cracks in the half-closed shutters and the musty smell was pungent. I brought the bag of croissants to my nose to soothe my senses. I turned and saw Michele still standing next to the wide open door, he was leaning with his shoulder against the door frame, staring at me with his arms folded.

"Are you not coming in?" I asked him without taking my nose out of the bag.

"Do you like it?"

"Um... no?" I didn't mean to offend him. By that point I'd understood where he had taken me and I was honestly wondering why. But it was one thing not to offend him, another one was to pretend that the house was beautiful. Even if I wanted to, I would never be able to pretend I liked it. Michele laughed amused, closed the door and walked past me to open the shutters. With the light breaking in the room the house looked different. Not beautiful, but less spoiled.

He slipped into one room and then reappeared and disappeared again in another. Finally, when he had opened all the windows, the light was really strong.

"Meet my house," he said with a proud face.

I looked at it again, turning my head from right to left and from bottom to top. I did not know what to say.

"It's the auction house, right?"

"It's my house."

"Yes, I understand it's your house, but it's the one you won at the auction, isn't it?"

"The auction only rightfully allowed me to take it back. These are the walls that have been my home more than any apartment I have ever lived in throughout my whole life."

"I don't understand, sorry, did you live here?"

"Yes, as a child. I was born here, in that room." He pointed to my right. "My mother was from Barcelona and lived in this house with her parents. Then she met my father and got pregnant with me. I lived here with her and my grandparents for the first four years of my life."

"And your father?"

"When my parents met, my father had already

decided to return to Italy. He had come to Spain to start a business but it didn't go well and, before running out of all his savings, he shut it down." He took a deep breath, as if that strong smell wasn't a problem for him. "So when he learned that my mother was expecting a baby, he decided to go back to Italy alone to find work and, as soon as he had the money to support us, we would join him. It actually happened, in fact, but it took more than four years and when I left this house and my grandparents, I suffered a lot. Everyone told me that I would finally live with my dad, but unfortunately for me he was almost an imaginary figure. I talked to him on the phone every day but I rarely saw him and, even making an effort, I couldn't quite remember his face."

"Then? What happened to this house? How did it end up for auction?"

"My grandparents had to sell it because their retirement money wasn't enough to keep it, and at the time they sent some help to my mother and me. After them, inexplicably every owner of these walls ended up having to give them up. Financial problems, divorces, deaths, up to the last owner whose assets were foreclosed, I don't know why."

"Excuse the question, but with all these misfortunes did not you have the doubt that maybe the house is a bit, let's say... hostile?"

He smiled, and I fell in love with his face that didn't seem to know how to wear masks. "Actually, I always thought it was waiting for me. You know, in all these years I have never stopped getting information on who has lived here and, every time it was put up for sale, I counted my savings so I could come here and buy it back. But it was never enough and so I held off, watched someone else take it and waited for the house to kick them out. This house wants me as much as I want it."

I watched him tell that story and I could discern all the emotions that he was filled with. I saw sadness and despair, but also so much joy and satisfaction, I saw the love he felt looking around those walls.

"Would you like to show me what it was like?"

He took the cup of coffee from my hands and placed the bag on an abandoned wooden plank in the middle of the room. He took my hand and led me back to the front door. "The coat hanger and a small table with the telephone on it were here. Then continuing on you entered the dining room, down there on the right was the round table of polished dark wood and there, where we were talking a little while ago, was the brown leather sofa and in the summer I would stick to it like an insect on a windshield." It was wonderful to watch him relive his childhood and it was evident that he was enjoying himself. In those guises of a man/child I had not guessed it, but the more we were in there, the more I saw a complex and tremendously fascinating personality emerge in him.

He showed me the room where his grandparents slept, the one where he slept with his mother and finally the kitchenette which was nothing more than a long and narrow corridor in which not even a tiny table would fit.

"But you haven't seen my favorite room yet."

I looked around and counted the thresholds, we had already entered each visible space and, unless there was a secret passage in the wall, there couldn't be any other rooms in that house.

"Would you mind taking our breakfast?"

"No, of course, where are we going now?"

He went to the French window of what was once

the dining room and flung the glass open. Just like at the front door before, he made me go first repeating: "After you."

Out in the open air I was greeted by a breathtaking scene. From that terrace, which at first glance seemed larger than the whole house, you could see Barcelona in its entirety. I approached the outermost point to understand how far that spectacular view could extend. I felt Michele's body a few centimeters from my back, then with a gesture that brought him even closer he took my arm and pointed it in a specific direction. I narrowed my eyes to focus, fighting the excitement that his proximity and scent caused me, and I saw it. I couldn't believe it, we were high enough to see the towers of the Sagrada Familia. I had traveled a lot and seen unforgettable places, but I had the impression that this would forever remain my favorite place in the world.

In the beauty of that morning, with the city at our feet and the blue sky as our roof, sitting on the ground on the terrace of the house where Michele was born, we had breakfast.

He told me many funny anecdotes of which his grandfather was always the main character. I asked him how he could remember everything in such detail, having been only four years old when they left that house. He explained to me that he often came to visit his grandparents with his mother because that had always remained their real home.

"And now? Will you live here?"

"No, no, I wish", he replied smiling. "Now I want to renovate it and then..."

Something must have troubled him deeply because suddenly his gaze became dark and sad.

"Then?" I pressed on.

"The fact Anna is that... well... nobody knows I bought it."

"What do you mean?" I asked convinced I'd misunderstood.

"Alex knows, Federica knows, I know and you know."

"Lisa knows too."

"That's true, even if Lisa only knows I bought it but not the reason".

"Well, Mery knows too, I guess."

Michele looked down at the ground. "No, she doesn't."

"Is it a wedding present?" I asked, bowing my head in an attempt to catch his eye.

"It's not that. It's just that she wouldn't understand."

I couldn't believe it, had this man come to Spain a few months before the wedding to buy a house without telling his fiancée? What was happening to men all over the world?

"You mean, you've been hiding it from her?"

"I know it's bad, and after reading your husband's letter, I feel awful to admit this but... it's complicated."

Of course, but it's not like the whole world's lack of courage can hide behind this excuse.

I watched him keep his head down and play with the hem of his pants, he seemed deeply troubled.

"More than bad I would say that it is... serious. Try to explain better."

"The fact is, I've been after this house for a lifetime. And I've never had a chance to afford it. When I saw it on the real estate auction site, I knew this had to be the right time. Now or never, you know?" I nodded and he continued: "But my financial situation hadn't changed, I had a comfortable life but I didn't have enough money to buy a house on Rambla de Catalunya. I had thought about a mortgage, but Mery did not agree to go into debt with the bank since we would soon have to ask for a loan to buy our house. So I put the idea aside for the umpteenth time. But I couldn't rest, every day I checked if the house was still on the market or if it had been sold. Mery was concerned about how much this matter was bothering me and asked me to stop thinking about it. Time to *close the chapter*, she told me."

He gave a sad smile, something I had never seen before. In a moment of deep empathy, I was able to feel what he was feeling. "I realized she was right, it made no sense to keep hoping. And for the first time I stopped following the fate of this house. The thought returned not long after, when my mother died. I had really wanted to bring her back here again once more in her lifetime. And I tormented myself at the thought of not having succeeded. Then something absurd happened: one afternoon a notary office called me and told me that my mother had written a will. I had no idea. I went to the meeting and found that she had amassed a small fortune over the years. It was my legacy since my father died years ago."

"So you looked for the house and saw that it was still up for auction?"

"Not right away, at first I was stunned by that news and, don't ask me why, I didn't even tell Mery."

"Are you joking? Didn't you tell her about the inheritance?"

"Let me finish, please. I had the money, I could do many things. They could be useful for our future, to create a family, to start a new business. But the more I thought about it, the more I realized that there was nothing that interested me more than this house. Could I have told Mery? Yes. Would she have understood? No."

"You can't know that." I stepped back with my hands resting on the floor behind me.

"Let's just say I know, because we've talked about it sometimes. They were far-fetched conversations like, *'If you won the lottery what would you do?'* I always replied that, first of all, I would buy the house in Barcelona and she called me crazy, then in the end she said: *'Luckily it will never happen'.*"

"You're right, they are far-fetched scenarios. It is quite different to secretly buy a house. After all, it's your money, isn't it? Don't you have the right to spend it as you see fit?" I stopped after saying those words, recognizing in the way I was expressing myself the pattern of keeping separate lives that Lorenzo and I had. That is actually not how it works when you are married, generally you put everything on the table and often the dealer wins. Bills, rents, mortgages, taxes, savings and earnings all end up in that vortex. Whether they belong to one or the other often no longer makes any difference. They weren't married but on that aspect they might as well have been. In any case, I found it inconceivable that he had done everything behind his fiancée's back.

"Where does she think you are now?"

"Here, celebrating my bachelor party."

"And didn't she get suspicious, in your opinion?"

"Undoubtedly, she expects me to come look at the house, otherwise she doesn't. It's quite normal that I chose to come to this city, she knows how fond I am of it."

Just because she knows you should be able to tell her, I told myself. But the matter was delicate and above all it was their business.

"Listen, Miky... why did you bring me here?" The question came out without my being able to control it, I had been wondering since we entered that house but I didn't think I could get it out.

Michele sighed and, pushing back, leaned against the wall. He was sitting in front of me with his knees bent and his feet flat on the ground, his arms wrapped around both legs and his hands tightly wrapped around each other.

"I'd like to ask you not to ask me." He hesitated for a moment. "But let's try this. The first time I wanted to bring you here was yesterday for lunch. When you left the club crying, I wanted to run after you and hug you. I wanted to make you feel protected and I thought about this place, you know, because of it makes me feel."

I looked at him and got the impression that he was answering to himself as well.

"I asked Alex not to come with me to get the keys."

It surprised me, I really didn't understand that hidden plot. At that point the questions I wanted to ask him were many more but I decided to follow his story. "Why did you change your mind then?"

"Because I wasn't sure it was right. So when you suggested we go to Guell I let things take their course."

"I never asked you to take me there... I just asked you how far it was."

"Well, let's just say I used it as an escape route. The fact is that last night I could not find peace. I cursed myself for not asking you and the more I thought about it the more I wanted to take you there. So, on impulse, I got into a taxi and came to you. I saw the room number on the keychain you were holding the other afternoon. As I stood in front of your bedroom door I felt like a real jerk. I was wondering what you would think of my proposal, I was sure you would say no. Plus Alex didn't even know I was out and he was waiting for me for our evening out. So I went down to the reception, asked for a pen and paper and wrote that note. I didn't want to leave like that, however, without telling you anything, I knew I would regret it and so I knocked on the door. You didn't open and I slipped the ticket under it." As if he'd snapped back to reality, he looked at me and smiled. "Sorry, I'm digressing."

"You are answering a lot of my questions. And how did we finally get here?"

"This morning I couldn't take it anymore, I spent the night tossing and turning, the thought of not seeing you again tormented me. In the end I followed that thing."

I looked at him frowning "What thing?"

"The thing that I can't explain, but that leads me to you." In the silence that followed our eyes remained fixed on each other, as if hooked, and what happened next was simply the inevitable. With a sure and delicate gesture he took my face in his hands and got closer until he touched my skin. He paused for a moment before touching to look at me, then kissed me. Not for a second did I want to resist that kiss. The warmth of his mouth, the scent of his skin, everything about that man captured and overwhelmed me. Finally raising my arm I sank my fingers into his wonderful, incredibly soft black hair.

16

Back to the hotel I sat on the bus, got on the first one I could find and I wasn't sure if it was going in the right direction. After that kiss there were no more words, we sat embracing in the silence of our thoughts. Thoughts, mine, which had quickly turned into confusion and bewilderment. I felt the urge to leave that wonderful terrace a stone's throw from the sky and escape, run and leave behind all the difficult things that I would have to face. Separating from Michele, first of all.

I had left him in his *new old* home, and when he had said goodbye, tenderly stroking my cheek, I had struggled to hold back tears. That, I thought, would be the sweetest memory I would have of him.

The bus stopped right in front of the Sagrada Familia and I instinctively got off. I sat on the bench under the majesty of Gaudi's temple while spring flaunted its most beautiful colors. What was I going to do now?

Would I go home, to face a husband who had lied to me all those years by rub the truth he had kept from me in his face? But now I too had something to confess. I had kissed another man and, worse, I had fallen in love with him. Would I have told Lorenzo? And if I hadn't, with what courage could I have thrown his lie in his face?

A very fast thought crossed my mind forcing me to observe it, so fast that at first I did not understand it. It was a memory, but a long time had gone by and I tried to grasp it better. I rested my head in my hands. Slowly the words began to resurface and, after a few minutes, I was able to put the pieces together.

I took the phone from my bag and called Lisa. It was just past noon.

"Hi, would you like to join me at the Sagrada Familia?"

"The Sagrada Familia? Why?"

"So we can visit it before we leave."

"Yes, that's fine. You sound weird."

"Appendicitis."

"Do you have appendicitis?"

"Not me. Lorenzo had appendicitis as a boy. It was serious, something went wrong. I don't remember what, it's been a long time, we didn't know each other back then but I know he was hospitalized, he told me he had to have surgery several times."

"You might have a point. I'll join you."

Part Two

17

While the man with the broad shoulders and the hazelnut jacket stood in front of me, I stared at his back, but without seeing it. I was at the mercy of my thoughts, victim of a tangle of emotions difficult to unravel, to understand individually. One above all, however, seemed dominant: fear. Why was I afraid? I thought I would feel curiosity, satisfaction, enthusiasm, but fear? Fear of what? I wondered listening to the heartbeat that seemed to come out of my chest. It was so strong that I had the impression it hurt. We were still on the stairs and that small taste had already evoked a flood of memories. When my grandmother told me to stay on the side of the wall because the railing wasn't safe, I watched her lean against the handrail and wonder, *if it's not safe why is she leaning on it?* Or when I came home and climbed those steps trying to take three with a single step at first it was difficult but then, when I was older, I was good at it, sometimes I was even able to slip into a set of four. I smiled at those still vivid glimpses. Finally, after trying several keys, the man managed to open the door. The blood throbbed in my body rhythmically, I could hear it running. Fear was becoming more and more dominant, and only when I was in the center of the hall did I let a breath out. The pungent smell of wet dog penetrated my nose, forcing me to protect it with my arm. The first impact was violent, the memory that I had kept untouched all those years was very far from what was in front of my eyes. In that instant I understood why I was scared. It was fear of being disappointed, I had waited, dreamed, longed for that moment my whole life and the expectation, alas, was very high. Besides, I was doing something really crazy by buying that house without telling my fiancée. And this increased the load. Once in there Mery would understand - I told myself - and not only that, she would also be happy to own property on one of the most famous streets in Barcelona. Looking around, however, I realized that before I could play the good investment card, I would have to dip into my savings to properly renovate those four walls. It was an unexpected event, it is true, but it certainly would not have stopped me.

All that was left of the house I remembered and of which I still felt the heat was the floor, opaque, encrusted, but nothing a good polish wouldn't easily offer its former glory. The tile pattern was certainly old-fashioned and not very similar to current interior design magazines, but I could never have covered it or replaced it with something else. The rest was a real disaster: peeling walls, damp stains and mold on their corners, the window frames were shabby, the doors non-existent.

Did they take the doors away?

A few light spots on the walls indicated the presence of paintings that had also been taken away, as was much of the furniture. I searched the rooms. On the wall the sign of the headboard indicated that the arrangement of the furniture had not changed over the years; I slept in that room with my mother and with my head resting on the pillow I could see the leaves of the weeping willow in the inner courtyard from the window. My grandparents' room, on the other hand, had been painted pink, a sign that it had hosted a little girl, I thought. I crossed the hall again to reach the kitchenette. I was surprised to see that the furniture, the one my grandmother had chosen by spending most of her savings, was still there: in over thirty years it had never been replaced by any owner. The image of the stovetop full of pots, one for each stove, and of my grandmother standing with her hands covered in flour enveloped me immediately, opening the gates to emotions that I had kept under control since I entered. I let my eyes fill with tears and my feelings take over, sorry I didn't have a door I could close behind me. The man with the keys had gone down to the street to give us more privacy, he had said, besides at that time in Spain you could take a *siesta*.

Lisa, after taking a quick look at the property, had also excused herself to make business calls. Setting foot in the living area, I tried to mentally reconstruct the old furniture: the round dark wood table on my right, the leather sofa in the center, the desk leaning against the back wall. Grandfather appeared to me sitting in the rocking chair next to the window, holding his fishing journal in his hand and reading it while smoking his pipe. I raised my hand and greeted him, grateful for having been able to "see him again". I looked forward to reliving memories of my mother: I wanted to see her young, happy, smiling as I had always seen her as a child when we lived in this house. Who knows how many worries were hidden behind that smile. I couldn't imagine at the time, but as I became an adult I learned that often the bigger the smile the heavier the worry load. No chance, my mother did not want to show herself. Alex, who until then had been a silent chaperone, knew the whole story well and granted me the space I needed. He had already set foot there, where I hesitated to go, the place that was the scene of all my best memories. Did I want to relive them? Undoubtedly. But it wasn't going to be easy. A happy past can hurt as much as a sad one, sometimes more, especially if you stop to think that, it is actually gone and past and will never be able to return. I crossed the threshold of the French window and found myself on the terrace. The light was the same as it was then, even the blue sky above my head was as I remembered it. The large wrought iron table and four chairs were missing, my grandmother's colorful flowers, all my toys and, above all, my mother's easel, her canvases. I quickly turned my head to the far right corner where she sat painting and saw her. In one hand the brush and in the other the palette, her look alternating between the canvas and the infinity. Her hair was gathered and held together by a brush that only she was able to wedge in to support the fullness of her hair. Her hands were stained with red and green, blue and yellow. Did she use the brush or her fingers? I had always wondered. She was as beautiful as I remembered her, she was my mom and her alone, her vision, was worth all the time I had waited. Yes, I told myself, even the lie I had told Mery.

I had reached the top, the climb had been very hard but I had made it. It would be all downhill from there. Telling Mery was the last hurdle before I could finally live my dream to the fullest.

18

"Earth to Miky, Earth to Miky. Oh no, heck, we're in the air. Air control to Miky."
"Why are you saying 'heck' now?"
"Adele made me swear not to swear anymore."
"Yes, but you're talking to me, not your daughter."
"I know, but it's not that simple, I have to keep at it, you know, it's like quitting smoking, just take a puff every now and then and you'll fall back into the habit immediately."
"I get it", I said, turning back to the window, my gaze lost on the white clouds stretching out before me.
"Anyway I wanted to tell you it's a pleasure to travel with you, you make me laugh."
Only Alex could manage to get a laugh out of me in that state of apathy. I turned back to my friend who was looking at me waiting for some explanation.

y, my head is elsewhere."
re is it? Where is your head? On Rambla de
a?"
ay."
"Are you thinking about how to tell Mery?"
"Tell her what?"
"What do you mean 'what'? You bought the house! Pal, what's the matter with you?"
"I'm not thinking about the house."
"What is it, a quiz? Is there a prize if I guess right?"

I dropped my head back on the seat. Alex kept looking at me as if I were making fun of him with those evasive answers, it was obvious that he didn't understand what I was talking about. What was clear in my head was not so clear to him who, despite having seen me disappear several times in that short vacation, had never asked me anything.

He did not know what I had felt that afternoon in the taxi when Anna slept on my shoulder, nor that after reading her husband's letter I wanted to hold her close to me and tell her that I would never do that to her, or the emotion I felt when welcomed her to my house that morning. He did not know that I had kissed her on the terrace and that our kiss had been incredible, I had desired it, I had dreamed of it, I believed it was wrong until it happened and, from that moment on, I was unable to think of anything else.

She had left and I had stayed there, sitting on my terrace breathing what was left of her perfume on me.

"I think I fell in love with her," I said without opening my eyes.

"In love with her... with... Anna?"

I nodded.

"How is that possible?"

"I don't know."

"Dude, you need to help me understand. If you don't want to talk about it, that's okay, but if you want to, you have to be a little more specific."

"I kissed her." I sighed.

"Ooookay", Alex said, staring at the seat in front of him. "It's certainly not a detail to be overlooked, however… I don't think it's appropriate to jump to conclusions. Don't underestimate the fact that the wedding is approaching and, even if it doesn't seem like it, tension builds, it's inevitable. You know you lied to Mery about the house and it certainly makes you anxious, because now you have to tell her and it's not easy." He sighed and looked at me again. "I don't want to say it's not important but… don't you think it could have been just a moment of weakness? Surely you felt something for that woman, but believing you fell in love with her…"

"I showed her the house."

Alex stared at me with wide eyes and an open mouth and then put his head back on the seat, staring at the plane ceiling. "That's a problem."

He knew it, he knew what it meant to me, he knew that I had hardly talked about it to anyone and that it had been my reason for living for years, he knew that I only wanted to share it with the few who had access to the deepest, most intimate and sometimes most unsure part of me. He knew that gesture meant much, much more than the kiss.

Why had I brought her there? Why hadn't I been able to get her out of my head since the day she passed out in my arms? I wanted to show her that house, share my story with her, tell her who I was, who I really was. I was Miguel, even if everyone called me

Michele because I had grown up in Italy and I was Italian for all intents and purposes, but being there, within those walls, I had seen the child I once was and who had remained trapped there for all those years, I had finally found him and with him my desire to laugh, to play, to run, to love. That was how I felt and that was how I wanted to be forever. But Miguel had stayed behind in Spain this time too, he had remained on that terrace because he had found what he was looking for there and that's the only place he wanted to be. Meanwhile I was going back to the place where everyone thought I was Michele and where I too, over time, had started using that name.

When we arrived at Fiumicino airport we went to get the car, and during the rest of the trip Alex tried to lighten the load that was crushing me and that he too had understood by now. He asked me to explain how things had gone but my answers were scattered, I was confused and my telling the story was a reflection of that.

"When will you see Mery?" he asked me when Perugia was a few kilometers away.

"Tomorrow night."

"Well, you have some time to recover."

Getting to my house, he pulled over by the sidewalk and I got off to grab my suitcase. Approaching the open window, I leaned down to say goodbye. "Do you want to come up?" I suggested seized by a sudden sense of anguish at the idea of going in alone.

"I can't, my permit is about to expire and I have to go get Adele." Then, scanning my face, he added: "Do you want to come with me?"

"No, it's fine, enjoy your little girl."

"Don't worry, Miky, it'll pass."

"I hope so." I patted the roof of the car as you do

the shoulder of a friend when you greet them and, dragging my trolley, I walked towards the front door.

19

Mery would ring the bell at any moment, while I was setting the table I tried to build a lineup of topics that would keep me active and talkative for the duration of the evening. I could not afford distractions, I could not let my mind wander as it had all day always bringing me back to her. Anna. She had conquered an infinite space inside me occupying my every thought and only sometimes I was able to block that flow, forcing me to concentrate on work.

Mery would certainly have asked me about the house, so I had to decide how to answer so as not to make her suspect anything. If I had denied having gone there, for example, she would have certainly understood that I was lying. My plans prior to this trip included me telling her the truth, once I returned after winning the house. The how was a detail I would have thought of once I got the result of the auction.

Destiny, however, had a different plan and during

those days my head had gone off on a different tangent. Moreover a strange thing had happened: as soon as I entered that house, the first time around with Alex and Lisa, my will to share it with Mery was already gone. It was something deeply personal that held me back from wanting to bring my newly rediscovered world into everyday reality. In Michele's life.

The doorbell rang and I went to the intercom to open the door.
As she climbed the stairs I took a deep breath and breathed out, hoping to release some tension as well. I looked at myself in the mirror hanging on the entrance wall and, forcing a smile on my face, I opened the door.
"Welcome back!" Mery said spreading her arms.
"Thank you", I replied, welcoming her into mine. When we got closer to kiss, however, I felt the urge to walk away. I tried not to convey my discomfort and was relieved when she said, "I brought the wine, although I guess sangria is running through your veins now."
I took her hand and grabbed the bottle. "Well, you know, not too much."
"Yeah, right, anyway I'm all ears."
"Let's go to the table, then, we'll talk better with our mouths full."
Mery looked at me with a raised eyebrow as she always did when I would say something stupid. She asked me how our time there had been, if the weather had been nice, if we had gone to the beach and if we had found a girlfriend for Alex. No reference to the house. This helped a lot in following the lineup of topics I had mentally prepared, so the dinner went by easily. How did it feel to be next to her now that

another woman had overturned all my certainties and led me to do something I never thought I could do? I thought that I would feel like scum, that she would be able to read the guilt on my face, I thought it would be difficult to be *Mery's boyfriend*, as I always had been. Instead how I felt for her was very similar to how I'd always had. Of course, it was strange to know that I had kissed another woman, but Mery was Mery, with her smile and her self-confidence that had always fascinated me.

After dinner we moved to the sofa to watch a movie on TV, that evening Mery was going to stay over even if it was Monday.

She lived in a small town fifty minutes from Perugia and, although we had been together for a long time, we had kept our respective houses in order to be comfortable at work. Mery, in fact, worked in an accountancy firm a few meters from her home and loved her apartment. I knew it would be a sacrifice for her to move to the city, but when someone asked her what she was going to do after the wedding, she always replied, *"With a ring on my finger and a bigger study, I might like it the same."*

For that reason, we usually spent Saturdays and Sundays at mine or hers, while during the week we only saw each other when she didn't leave work too late and I would join her at her house to have dinner together.

This is the moment I could talk to her about the house, I thought encouraged by the relaxed atmosphere, I could not have hoped for anything better actually. However, I pushed back the thought not wanting to stir things up.

I let the evening pass quietly and, later in bed, we made love with our usual ease. Of course I would never have imagined it thinking back to how tense I was about seeing Mery again. Before turning off the light on the bedside table, I looked at my girlfriend sleeping next to me, brushed her black hair away from her face, smiling at her funny expression. I still found her beautiful, her skin was smooth and, apart from a couple of wrinkles at the edge of her eyes, she did not look thirty-eight years old. Since she had cut her hair, she had looked about ten years younger.

Lucky her, even if we are the same age I look much older.

I sighed enjoying that moment of peace. "Don't worry, it'll pass", said Alex.

Maybe he was right.

20

"I've made an appointment for two o'clock on Saturday afternoon, is that okay for you?" Mery asked me on the phone.

It was Thursday and we were planning weekend engagements as I drove to the university, silently cursing the morning traffic. I was going to give a lecture that seemed too heavy to me, let alone the kids. The thought of how to try and make the lesson more interesting distracted me from the imaginary calendar Mery was listing for me.

"I'm sorry, I wasn't following... appointment for what?"

"For the house, let's go check out the attic I e-mailed you the other day. Do you remember?"

"Yes, yes, of course... the attic. Didn't we say it's a bit beyond our reach? "

"Actually you said it... and anyway my parents want to give us a hand, so I'd like to take that into consideration."

"As you like, the time is fine."

"After that I was thinking of asking the real estate guy if we can go to the agency, so he can show us what's available, okay?"

"It's not necessary, we have already asked Alex to keep us updated on the properties in the area."

"Yes, but you don't want to only lean on him, do you? What's wrong with consulting other agencies?"

"Nothing, but I'd like to find a property through him."

"If he is able to find what we are looking for, then so be it."

Objecting was useless.

The week had gone by quite normally. The newfound confidence I had felt the first night with Mery had not been a constant, but it had played well against the snapshots of Anna's sweet face that my mind treacherously projected. They surprised me at the most unexpected moments, while I was writing an equation on the blackboard, while mixing sauce for pasta, when I was standing in line at the bar to have a coffee. Each time it was the same shot, I had to stop to assimilate it, take a deep breath before starting again. I wasn't the one looking for those memories, on the contrary, if I happened to think of her, for example, at night before going to sleep, I always tried to reject her image, I tried not to fall prey to that dangerous memory. But I had to at least live with those frames until the mind would have exhausted them. I also had other problems to deal with: within a few days the renovations of the house in Rambla de Catalunya would begin and, in addition to not having told Mery yet, I had to think about how to get there again. There was no way out, I would have to tell her about it that weekend.

"The house is very bright as it faces entirely south and, as you can see, the spaces are large enough to create a couple more rooms." The real estate agent spoke as I looked around wondering what the hell we were doing there. The house was beautiful, sure, but it was excessive for our needs, both in terms of cost and of space. We didn't need four bedrooms, even six, if we had followed the suggestion of the guy in the suit and tie.

"We could make this a study," Mery considered leaving me even more troubled by the fact that she, on the other hand, was taking it seriously.

"For who?"

"For you, to prepare your lectures."

"I've always prepared them on the kitchen table, I don't need a study."

"Yes, but you're not the only one who's going to live in the new house, maybe I might need to use the kitchen table."

I realized that we were entering a minefield and I preferred to just let it go.

After the visit we went to the agency where, sitting at the desk, the realtor turned the computer monitor towards us to show us the numerous options available at that time. All, needless to say, like the attic we had just viewed.

It bothered me to waste that sunny Saturday looking at houses we would never buy but, all in all, it was better this way: at least Mery would no longer object to letting Alex take care of everything.

When we were done, I asked her what she wanted to do, it was almost five p.m. and we decided to go downtown. In the car, stuck in traffic that I found unusual for a Saturday, Mery asked me what I thought of the house.

"Which house?" I replied.

"The house we've just seen, remember?" Her tone was sarcastic and slightly annoyed.

"Sorry, the realtor showed us a million on the computer. It's beautiful, but I would say far from what we are looking for. Right?"

"Why are you saying this?"

I remained silent, pondering the most suitable words to use. It seemed absurd to me I even had to explain, but it was clear that we were looking for a house with very different points of view.

"It looks incredibly big to me and, for the cost, we would really have to tighten our belts."

"Well, everyone does."

"Who's 'everyone'?"

"Everyone, everyone who gets married and buys a house has to tight their belts for the first few years."

"Okay, but if we had the opportunity to buy a less giant house and enjoy life without always having to think about not spending more than what is strictly necessary, wouldn't it be better?"

"Then let's stay in your studio apartment so you can enjoy life!"

I was surprised by her arrogant tone and the hostile position she had assumed by crossing her arms. I thought I had been reasonable in expressing my point of view.

"Well, I think there could be more than a happy medium between my house and the 'Royal Palace of Caserta' we're talking about," I replied. I didn't want to argue but, at the same time, I was annoyed by Mery making a scene. She fell silent, staring out the window with her arms folded.

"I don't want to go downtown anymore, let's go home, please," she said suddenly breaking the silence treatment she had reserved for me. Her childishness freaked me out.

"I hope you're joking? We are almost there and it took us half an hour to cover thirty meters! " I blurted out.

"I don't care, I don't want to walk, the guys will be there too and I'm not in the mood."

"Well, if you don't mind, I am, I have been indulging your absurd wishes for three hours, now I'm going to indulge mine. You don't want to go downtown? Great." I turned the car around and headed for my house. Once we arrived, I pulled over a few meters" from the gate and, without turning off the car, remained motionless with my hands resting on the steering wheel.

"Aren't you coming?" Mery asked obviously surprised by my rebellious gesture.

"No, I'm going back to the center."

She stared at me for a few seconds. The clicking of the blinker marked the time.

With a sprint she got out of the car and slammed the door shut.

"Isn't Mery here?" Federica asked after greeting me with a kiss on the cheek.

"She was tired." Without any desire to explain, I got away with that excuse.

"Are we talking about the fact that you and Mister Realtor over there at the counter promised me we would celebrate your bachelor party together this weekend?" my friend scolded me.

"I'm here for this reason."

A smile lit up her face. Alex saw me from inside the

pub and nodded to me to ask if I wanted a cocktail. I said yes, raising my thumb and waving my hand to tell him to get some food too. The place was crowded, inside you could see a sea of heads and glasses held high by those who hurried out, carrying their drink to safety.

After a few minutes, my friend emerged from the crowd with signs of fatigue on his face.

"Thank you, friends, for coming to my aid."

"We had to keep the table"

"Welcome man, where is your sweetheart?"

"Home," I replied in an involuntarily annoyed tone.

"Mhmm... you must have liked the houses," Alex retorted with his usual way of lighten the mood when I was angry.

"You wouldn't understand."

"Oh no no, I can understand perfectly, I know the agency you contacted."

"It was Mery, you know I would never betray you."

"Miky is here to celebrate his bachelor party" Federica intervened, interrupting our debate. Alex gave me an inquisitive look, he knew that Mery had not come to Perugia to be alone at my house on a Saturday night.

I winked at him.

"Great!" he said patting me on the leg. "What do you want to do?"

"Dinner and the club?" Federica suggested.

"Come on, Fede, you and clubs. Enough, you're no longer young, get over it," Alex retorted.

"I'm actually thirty years old and I'm young enough, but I understand that old people like you can no longer stand frenetic rhythms."

"How are you thirty? You were thirty when I met you!"

I stayed silent to enjoy the dialogue I knew by heart by then because I had already heard it a thousand times, but each time it seemed more fun.

"When you met me you were thirty years old."

"Yeah... and you looked my age."

"Look, you really are a bastard! However, I am much younger than you and this is indisputable."

"Okay, kid... then we'll take you home and have the evening to ourselves. Like old men, okay?"

"Don't you dare, I've already forgiven you for Barcelona. So, let's just have dinner so you can tell me how it went!"

Alex and I exchanged a knowing look that did not go unnoticed. "I'll rephrase that," she said, "let's go to dinner because you absolutely have to tell me about Barcelona!"

"Okay," I replied, "but let's go to a quiet place where we can talk without having to scream over the music."

"Oh dear, boys, you are zombies!" Federica snorted.

After happy hour we tried booking a table for dinner, but restaurants that evening seemed to have been stormed and the best places were full. In the end it was Alex who saved the evening with his proposition. "Let's go to the best restaurant in town," he said.

"Which would be?" Federica asked.

"My house."

"Exciting, are we having a sleepover with Adele?"

"It's her mother's birthday and she's sleeping at hers tonight."

Although two years had gone by, I still found it

strange when Alex, speaking of Giorgia, said things like "her mother", "my ex-wife". He hadn't called her by her given name since they split, as if he wanted to maintain a certain distance. On the one hand I understood him: he had suffered a lot because of her, and putting an imaginary distance between them had somehow helped him recover. But I still wasn't used to it anyway. When two people stay together for years, their names said one after the other sound like one. "AlandGio", "MikyandMery". "Alandhisex " was annoying to say.

As I drove to Alex's house, I pictured Mery alone in my house and wondered if she was still angry. I was annoyed, I had found her behavior unfair and childish, but the anger had subsided and I could not help but wonder if I'd been out of line leaving her that way. There was also another aspect that made me think, surely Mery must have also been amazed by a reaction I would never have done in the past. I would have certainly expressed my opinions, but I would not have brought her home and left her so easily. I could have tried reasoning with her, I could have been assertive, but I had been childish like she had by behaving like this. Maybe it would have been better to go home to her but, to be honest, I didn't want to.

Alex lived in a townhouse he had bought with Giorgia before their wedding. For a time after the separation he had been looking for something smaller, arguing that he didn't need three floors to live alone in with his daughter. The reality was that living in there reminded him of the weight of his marriage failing. But when he had found a property suitable for his needs, he had pulled back just before signing the agreement. From that moment he had learned to love those walls in which, day after day, he saw his little girl grow up and he had confided in me that, when he saw her play in the garden, he thought about how beautiful it was to still be there.

"Come on, guys, who's spilling the beans?" Federica asked, rolling up the spaghetti with her fork.

Alex and I exchanged a knowing look.

We told her things that never happened, going back and forth as if we had studied the part. We both added intriguing details that made it increasingly difficult to continue the story for the other who took over, and regularly at the best part we stopped talking by driving Federica crazy, insulting us and throwing pieces of bread at us.

"So that's it? You're cutting me out?"

I went up to her and put my arm around her shoulders, ruffling her hair with my other hand. "No, little girl, now we'll tell you everything."

"Everything everything?" my partner in crime intervened.

"Everything", I replied, "there are no secrets between us three."

Federica had been in our group for several years; when Alex had separated and was left alone with his little girl she had been very close to him, she often went to his house to play with Adele and keep her company when her father was in despair. I too went there often, so the three of us had bonded to the point of almost becoming siblings.

We told her about the auction, about the night at the club celebrating my bachelor party, about the house, what it was like and how I imagined it would become. I showed her the photos I had taken.

"You mean you busted our balls for a lifetime for this rock pile?" she said with a wink. "I'm so happy for you! You really deserve it! Now... let's talk about serious business. Why do I have the feeling th more?"

"Because you're a woman and you have th sixth sense!" Alex retorted, rolling his eye exhausted expression.

"There's more, but let's get comfortable."

I poured wine into her glass and topped up the other two. We moved to the couch, taking the glasses with us. I told her the whole story without leaving out any detail, I told her I met Anna at a supermarket checkout while she was trying to pay for her sunscreen, I told her about her back which seemed to glow from behind even if it was covered by her T-shirt, I talked about the coffee, how her work fascinated me, her fainting. Federica opened her mouth when she heard me say that the next day I had found her in front of the restaurant when I had dragged Alex to the beach of Barceloneta in the hope of meeting her "by chance". I told her about Lorenzo's letter and I saw how sorry she felt for Anna, I told her about the goodnight note under the door and finally about the morning in Rambla de Catalunya, which ended with us kissing on the terrace. Listening to the whole story, Federica let herself fall backwards, lying on the armchair with her hands covering her face.

"I can't believe you are the protagonist of this story!" she whispered staying still. "You don't do these kinds of things! You are the perfect man!"

"Miky? The perfect man? What goes on in a woman's mind? Is that what you talk about when twenty-seven of you go to the bathroom together?"

"Only after discussing your bald head."

Alex ran his hand over his head, proudly stroking the smooth skin.

"Admit it, Father Michele shocked you this time," I

said with a wink.

She sat up quickly. "You were with them when I called!"

"Yes, and you were on speakerphone."

"What does this woman look like? Besides her green eyes, I mean, you've talked enough about those."

"Nice legs, long enough and nice strong hips," was Alex's description.

"Did you have the opportunity to look at her upper part too?" Federica gave my poor friend a disapproving look. "And I'm not talking about her boobs."

He raised his hands in surrender.

"She's quite tall," I said. My mind went back to the day I first met her. "She has long, dark hair but I couldn't figure out if it is brown or red, it looks chocolate but if you look at them in the sun it's a deep red. She has bangs but not short, it frames her eyes, she has some small freckles on her face. Very light complexion, almost transparent. Physically she's like you."

"Like me… how? Be careful how you answer."

"Like you in the sense that she is neither thin nor fat, she has a nice body, you both do, but you are not extremely thin, you are two soft beauties."

Having overcome that moment of amazement and curiosity, Federica asked many questions about my feelings for Anna and equally about what I felt for Mery. She, compared to Alex, seemed more open to asking questions, to questioning me about the origin of those emotions, of those feelings. And also of the gestures that, as she claimed, would not belong to me if not for someone really special. At first I was afraid she would judge me for kissing another woman. I thought she would instinctively take Mery's side out of female solidarity. Instead, she surprised me by showing concern because my fiancée was in danger of marrying a man with uncertain and confused feelings.

That's what she made me reflect on. I kept telling myself that things would soon return to normal, that I would be able to forget Anna and love Mery for my whole life, but that's not what I felt at that moment. What if it wasn't as simple as I had hoped?

21

Sunday morning I waited for Mery to come out of the bathroom wondering if she was still angry or if, like me, she wanted to forget what had happened the previous day. I made the coffee and filled two cups. The light seemed unable to filter the dull grey clouds that obscured the sky and a few drops of rain were already falling on the window panes.

My house was as Mery had described it: a studio apartment.

However, it was much larger than what that label might suggest, in real estate jargon they call it a loft. The sloped roof gave the room different sizes, in the upper part the wall reached four meters and I had built a mezzanine in which I had built the bedroom. In the lower part was the white, linear kitchen, with an island in front on which I often ate, especially when I was alone. Turning your back to the kitchen, there was an immense open space room starring the glass table, with steel legs that formed a figure similar to an ice crystal. I immediately liked it when I saw it displayed in the showroom of the furniture store but then, once I got home, it seemed too formal. Fortunately, the wooden floor and ceiling made it very welcoming.

Beyond the dining area was the corner sofa - on which I often ended up falling asleep - the TV on the opposite wall and a bookcase that took up the entire wall next to it. In the lower part of the house I could stand comfortably by raising my arms to touch the beams.

"You came home late, I fell asleep waiting for you", Mery said taking her cup.

"I was at Alex's. I'm sorry about how things went yesterday."

"I didn't think you were really going to leave," she said, looking at me. "I sat on the couch with my jacket on for half an hour, convinced you would come back for me."

"I'm sorry", I repeated, "I overreacted, can we start over?"

Mery shrugged and continued talking, I had the impression that she had prepared her speech during the evening spent alone. "Do you know what infuriates me?" she asked me without any real interest in receiving an answer. "That you were willing to go into debt to buy that stupid house in Barcelona even though you knew we were looking for one for us. However, now that with the same amount of money we would have spent on two houses, we can buy a fabulous one... you don't feel like it anymore. I think you're very selfish."

I understood her point of view, and even though I didn't like the tone she was using, I tried to gloss over it. I knew I had a lot of things to make amends for and I certainly couldn't point the finger at her at that moment.

"I'm sorry you see it that way."

"It's that house's fault, isn't it?"

"What?"

"Have you been there last weekend?"

"Yes", I admitted, shaken by a quick shiver.

"I knew! I knew you would! You didn't listen to me, you had to go there anyway knowing that you would be tortured again and that you would have tortured me too!"

"If you knew that why are you so angry?" I didn't want to fight. I also had to be careful what I might say, a confession at that moment would have been fatal.

Mery dropped onto the couch, she seemed exasperated to have to talk about that story again, but then her face softened. "What was it like?"

I smiled at her, grateful for the hand she was holding out to me. "She was beautiful, she was destroyed but to me she was beautiful."

"What do you mean 'destroyed'?"

"All that was intact was the floor, the rest is completely falling apart."

"The floor?" she asked with a bewildered expression. "Are you saying you went in?"

Here was my house of cards starting to collapse. I wasn't going to be able to handle all those secrets and I knew it was time to tell her the truth. But she was so angry that I couldn't find the courage to make the situation worse. "Yes, I asked the curators of the auction if I could see it."

"Were you able to?"

"Apparently."

"I knew it, when you told me you were going to Barcelona to celebrate your bachelor party, I knew you were going there for that reason. And here we are now!"

"Here where?"

"Here, now, when you don't care anymore… about us, about the wedding, about our future life together. Now you'll only think about that stupid, stupid house again! I can't take always watching from the sidelines."

"Sidelines? What are you even saying? I've never put you aside."

"Do you really think so? Consider how many things we could have done if you hadn't set aside every penny of your salary over the past thousand years! Think about how many trips, how many romantic dinners I gave up to indulge your crazy wish. You always put that before everything else, but I've had enough. We are getting married in four months and I have no intention of ruining even this moment of my life."

I felt guilty of all those accusations. They were true, but in those years of saving for my dream I didn't realize she felt left out. I was doing it for us too, we could escape to our nest abroad whenever we had the opportunity and I always imagined that she would be happy. So why had I bought it without telling her? I was guilty, guilty of everything, including what she still didn't know. I felt miserable.

"Listen, Miky." Mery got up from the sofa, went to the bookcase and picked up some magazines. "I'm going back to my house, I need to calm down and I don't want to fight anymore." She came towards me and placed the material she was holding on the dining table, then she lifted my chin with her fingers. "Talk to you later, okay?"

I nodded and kissed her.

"I'll leave some of the things I've selected for our honeymoon here, take a look if you want to."

"I certainly will." I hugged her and whispered in a faint voice: "I'm sorry."

"Me too."

22

"We need to meet immediately, I've found the house for you and Mery," Alex exclaimed as soon as I answered my cell phone.

"I can't now, I have a lesson, is lunchtime okay?"

"Okay, I'll be waiting at your house."

When I finished the lesson I hurried home and, amazed not to find him at the gate, I went up to leave my backpack and freshen up. Alex was waiting for me at my apartment door.

"I thought I'd find you downstairs," I told him. "How did you come up?"

My friend triumphantly jingled a bunch of keys in front of my eyes and asked me to follow him. He took no more than three steps to the right and inserted the key into the lock.

It didn't take me long to figure out what he was about to offer me when, throwing open the door of the apartment adjacent to mine, I found it empty. It looked like one of those scenes in the movies, when the owner comes home and finds it completely burglarized. It was the exact mirror of the loft I lived in on the other side of the wall.

I looked at Alex who hadn't lost his proud expression.

"Should I buy this house? So we could live close but apart?"

"Truthfully, it wouldn't be a bad idea to keep your homes divided, I'm speaking from personal experience, but I was thinking of a large open space by knocking down the partition."

I looked around: like mine, the space was a loft and we shared the central wall. In the lower part, as on the other side, I was able to stand still having several centimeters available before touching the light wooden beams of the ceiling.

"Do you think it can be done? I mean tearing down that wall... it seems supporting."

"Friend, you do the math and I make the plans, to each their own."

He showed me his idea, asking me to imagine what it would have been like without that wall, raising a new one, extending the mezzanine, the sofa, the bedrooms, the two bathrooms...

At the end of his presentation I was delighted.

"Plus," he added, "it'll cost you a lot less than buying a whole house since part of it is already yours and, even with the cost of the renovation, you'll have some money left to go out with your best friend every Friday night."

"Ah, there's a conflict of interest here."

"Fair, but above all I thought that this way you could resume work in the other house."

That was a nice plus. After realizing that Mery was

planning to spare no expense for our new home, I had stopped the renovations on Rambla de Catalunya. A decision also made worse by the sense of guilt I felt for having spent so much money without my girlfriend knowing, my girlfriend who, I had concluded, should not have been the one to lose out in all of this. With that offer I could have pushed the two renovations forward at the same time.

"I like it!" I exclaimed, slapping my hand on Alex's shoulder, my friend looking at me as if I had beaten him up.

"Only thing left to do is tell Mery."

"Well, you can always tell her after you buy it," he teased me.

"Ah ah... how funny!"

"Seriously, I've devised a plan." As a true pro, Alex knew my girlfriend wouldn't even consider the idea if we brought her in there without a project. Mery had many qualities, but a vivid imagination was not among them.

He proposed to draw the design he had told me about and, while we were discussing it, he was enthusiastic and said: "Listen, why don't we go to my office and write down a render? It's much more convincing than a project, you'll see."

"Can you do it?I mean, I know it takes time to make a render and... well, you ask for good money for them."

"Among the many stupid questions I get asked when I wear work clothes, *'Can you do that?'* I hadn't heard from in years. Yes, since I'm the owner and head honcho of MY agency, I can do whatever the *hell* I want."

"Excellent, head honcho, I feel you're still good at following the orders of your *five-year-old!*"

"I'm second only to her."

We went to his office and, when our eyes came to no longer distinguish yellow from red, we had the render. The house would come out wonderful.

"How do you plan on showing it to Mery?"

"This is the plan: she's staying at my house tonight so early in the morning, like around eleven, you show up in front of my door with your laptop and, after showing her the project, we'll take her there. What do you say?"

"Great, noon okay? I wouldn't want to disturb you two before eleven," he said with a provocative smile.

Things went as expected, at first Mery was not enthusiastic about the proposal but when she barely managed to build the image of the finished house in her mind, she gave in. It was decided. We signed the agreement the same day and we only had to wait for the bank's technical deadlines to conclude the deed. The loan, which I made in my name for practical purposes, was almost useless at that point and took a few days to approve.

In mid-May construction began and I moved in with Alex for a while, as my apartment would also be part of the construction site.

From then on, things went back to normal. Mery, happy to have finally found a house, devoted herself to wedding planning: hairdresser, esthetician, dress, bridesmaids. All of which I was happy to be exempted from. Easter, which we had celebrated at her parents' house, had come and gone too and, even though I missed my mom and dad, I was grateful to be welcomed into what would soon become my new family.

I pushed away every thought about Anna until, as I had predicted, my mind ran out of images of her face to sucker punch me with. That kiss had been a mistake, in the end Alex had been right attributing it to a moment of weakness and now I was convinced too. Everything was going according to the plans that Mery and I had made.

23

Alex and Adele got home while I was baking chicken and potatoes. It was just past seven p.m. and, as always since I had moved to their house, I was making dinner.

"Hello beauty! Hello beast!"

Adele jumped into my arms. "Hi, Miky! How nice it is to come home and always find you here. It's like having a male mother." That sentence touched me even though she had said it with serenity. Adele's sweetness was inordinate and she possessed the great gift of friendliness which, combined with her tenderness, were the only characteristics she had inherited from her father. The rest of her was a photocopy of Giorgia. I hugged her tightly and gave her a dizzying spin which she accompanied with a howl. It was nice for me to be there too, even though I wasn't at home I hadn't even felt uncomfortable once during the last month.

"What did you cook?" she asked running to peek through the oven glass.

"Chicken and roasted potatoes."

"Dad, why don't you ever make chicken and roasted potatoes?"

"Because I don't have to repay anyone to live here."

Despite his silly jokes, I knew full well that Alex was happy with my being there.

The evening was mild and we had set the table in the garden taking advantage of the longer days.

"Did you start with the renovations in Barcelona again?" he asked, biting into a chicken leg.

"Not yet, I want to finish renovating this one first."

"Do you plan on telling her before the wedding?"

"I think I'll tell her after I remodel it."

Alex's strategic move to persuade Mery to buy the apartment next to mine had given me the idea of how and when to confess my secret to her. I would have done all the work, I would have made it beautiful and only then would I have brought my wife there.

"And are you planning on renovating it before the wedding?"

"Honestly, I doubt it. Why are you interested?"

"No reason, I'm thinking about your vows and I think it would be better to start with no secrets."

That thought surprised me and I was also surprised by the seriousness with which he had spoken. The man in front of me was not the usual joker, he seemed more like a father intent on giving the talk to his son.

Adele was playing ball on the lawn torturing Ginger, the cat, who had the unfortunate role of second player.

"What's the difference if I tell her before or after?

Definitely not her reaction."

"No, but this way you'll save your... butt."

"What do you mean?"

"Have you ever thought that Mery might leave you for such a thing?"

I looked at him with wide eyes. "Honestly, I haven't."

"Honestly?"

I took a loaf of bread and broke it in two with my hands. "I don't understand."

"I think you've actually thought about it. Maybe not consciously, but I don't believe you've never considered the problem. So you're going out of your way to wait after the wedding. This way, no matter how much she can yell, get angry and threaten you, she will no longer be able to do what scares you most: leave."

"Al, do you really think so?"

"If not, why haven't you told her yet?"

"It's complicated."

"Yes, of course... it's complicated. So many things are and from August on you will see how many will. The question is: how do you plan on dealing with them? Lying? Hiding the issues? Doing what you like behind the backs of those who love you? And the children?" On that last question he raised his tone.

"What children?"

"Yours. You'll have some, I suppose, and they can't suffer because of you. If you are not sincere now you never will be."

In that moment I understood that my friend was thinking about his own marriage, about what Giorgia had done to him and Adele. I felt my heart squeeze looking at that man still so furious with his ex-wife and, at the same time, always so loving with his daughter.

Alex apologized and told me he had ex but renewed the advice to speak with M the wedding. "The foundations of a marriage ɩ.. solid", he admonished me. He was right.

I took Adele to bed, since I was with them that little girl exploited me for everything that her father usually did, making me think that she really saw me as the maternal figure she lacked in that domestic picture.

When I went back downstairs, I found Alex still sitting in the garden. The table had been cleared and there were only two cans of beer, the coffee maker and two mugs on it.

"I didn't know if you wanted coffee or beer, so I got both."

"Thanks", I said, filling the cup. "Feel better?"

Alex sighed and, placing the can on the table, settled into his chair. "Usually it's not like that, you know, but then there are moments that..." He raised his hands in the air as if cursing the sky.

"Are you still suffering because of Giorgia?"

He laughed bitterly. "Not because of Giorgia."

"For Adele," I concluded.

He nodded. "She could have done even worse to me. I suffered, you know, but then - sooner or later, in one way or another - you get up and, over time, I even managed to think that I have only missed out on a vision I had. She wasn't who I thought she was. We weren't what I thought we were. But I can't forgive her for abandoning Adele. Now she wants to make up for lost time, she wants to see her, she calls me and always asks me about her. But I was there, looking her in the eye when she asked me where her mother was and why she didn't love her anymore."

She stopped to wipe away tears and I managed to

hold back mine.

"Good for you for letting Adele visit with her", I told him, noticing he couldn't get back on track.

"She's still her mother."

I nodded.

"If you had seen her that day, the first time she saw her again. She was excited, agitated, I couldn't even keep her calm to eat. She hadn't slept all night and had made me pull the best clothes out of her closet the day before. I looked at her and silently writhed in anger. A little girl shouldn't do so much to please her mother. A little girl shouldn't be afraid that her mother doesn't like her." He opened the second can of beer after making sure I didn't want it.

"She was only three years old..." I sighed, mentally retracing how much time had passed since then.

"Yes, three years old when we separated, then she came back a year later."

Giorgia had left Alex on a Saturday morning two years earlier, showing up with her suitcases packed and a letter in which she told him she had never stopped loving her ex-boyfriend. The same day she left, leaving her daughter who was still sleeping unaware in her bed and her husband ravaged by pain in the kitchen. When I got to his house, as quickly as possible, I found him breathing into a paper bag in a panic attack.

"Adele is a happy child and do you know why? Because you love her and you do your best to be the great dad you are."

"Do you know that the first few days after Giorgia left I was afraid she wasn't my daughter?"

"But luckily you realized she was already talking a lot of bullshit, so the father had to be you."

I found it in me to respond with that joke because I

had already been caught unprepared the first time he confessed it to me. Then I remember I had begun to build the image of Giorgia's new partner in my head, hoping not to find similarities with the little one. Then, perhaps due to how much pain that thought caused him, the doubt in Alex had died and he concluded that she could only be his. Plus, from the research I had done after Alex had told me what happened, it had emerged that the guy in question had lived abroad during the first three years of their marriage. This didn't completely rule it out, but it made it very unlikely.

That evening, lying in bed in the guestroom, I couldn't sleep. I was thinking back to what Alex had said on the foundations of a marriage. Reliving that painful story made me understand what my friend meant better. Free to wander, the thought went to Anna. She too was struggling with a weak pillar, one weakened by a lie just like the one I was carrying out. How had she faced Lorenzo on his return? Had she left him? Had she forgiven him? Had our kiss somehow affected one decision or the other? Had she confessed to him? One by one, the thoughts found space in my mind, and when I felt her image waiting to be pushed back, I gave up and let her in.

24

As I suspected, I didn't get a wink of sleep that night. As soon as Anna's face appeared in the dark I felt a strong heat in my chest and the desire to have her near, to be able to hold her in my arms once again, overwhelmed me. I felt an uncontrollable shaking in my legs like a need to get out of bed and run, run fast, run to her. It was enough to let my mind recall her face to relive the most beautiful moments we had spent together. I kept seeing her big eyes, her pink lips the moment before I kissed them, and then let imagination reinvent the sequel according to my desire. I imagined caressing her neck and move my hand down towards her breasts, I remembered the fruity scent of her skin and I imagined following the path of my hand with my mouth. I heard her sigh as I unbuttoned her blouse and wrapped my hands around her hips. I watched her arch her back and drop her head back as I kissed her chest and then her belly and, as I gently laid her down on the terrace floor, I felt her hand in my hair, first brushing it and then grabbing it hard while pleasuring her with my mouth. I imagined taking off her jeans and caressing her smooth legs while I too freed myself from my bulky clothes and then slowly leaning on top of her and enjoy the sensation of our bodies touching. I continued to love her under that blue sky and, hearing her labored breathing, increased the pleasure I felt with her.

That passion coursing through my veins prevented me from sleeping, from thinking, from understanding. All I felt was her inside of me and I didn't want anything else. It was wrong but it was out of my control.

At the first light of morning, the rising of a new dawn brought rationality back to my thoughts. As I watched the sky leave the darkness of the night and turn shades of pink and blue, I imagined Anna lying in her king bed next to her husband. I could not guess the features of that man, nor his body shape or guess his age, but picturing her there beside him left me motionless, surrendered. After all, if Anna had wanted to she could have looked for me, Lisa had my number. My thoughts ran at high speed and I suddenly realized that in Barcelona I had called Alex from Anna's cell phone. So I would have found Anna's number in Alex's phone. I jumped up and went down to the kitchen hoping to find him awake. It was Saturday and in a few minutes I would have to leave to go to Mery's.

Alex wasn't there, I tried the bathroom but no one answered. It was absurd, I realized it, but I couldn't wait. I went to his room and found him still asleep.

"Al, Al, wake up."

"What the hell do you want?" he answered in a

voice I had never heard from him before.

"Get up, I need your phone."

"Did something happen?" he asked turning to me suddenly awake.

"No, I just need a number you have on your phone."

"What number?"

"Anna's number." My friend looked at me with an expression that was a mixture of anger, weariness and disbelief.

"What are you saying?"

"Look, I'm sorry if I woke you up, I promise that if you turn on your phone and look at us later I'll let you sleep as long as you want."

From the next room Adele's voice made Alex's head fall back on the pillow knowing that, at least for the day, the time to be lazy was over.

"What time is it?" he asked me putting on the sweatpants that were previously leaning on the chair next to the bed.

"Half past seven... more or less."

"You know I hate you, right? And there is no haute patisserie breakfast that you can prepare that would make me forgive you."

"Where's your phone?" I asked impatiently.

"In the kitchen. I'll take Adele and go downstairs and then you can explain what the hell you came up with."

I waited a few minutes and took the opportunity to make the coffee. I set the mermaid glass and the teaspoon with the rainbow handle for Adele.

While the little girl ate her meal, I handed the cup of coffee to Alex who was leaning against the kitchen counter, waiting for the phone to turn on.

"Can you tell me what's wrong with you?"

"I don't really know, but I couldn't sleep and then it occurred to me that you must have Anna's number on your phone, in your incoming calls... and I didn't understand anything anymore."

"Gliding over what you're going to do with it... do you really think I still have her number on my incoming calls after two months? Okay, I might not be a man about town but I get phone calls too."

I did not consider that.

"So you're telling me you don't have it?"

"Tell me what you would like to do with it."

"I don't know."

"You don't know? I wish the reason that got me out of bed at half past seven on a Saturday was a little more significant."

I sat in the chair behind me, dropping my dangling arms. What would I have done if he had had that number? What had pushed me in that last half hour to want to get it at all costs? I didn't have an answer.

Perhaps that daydream had taken me to the point that I no longer remembered where my life was at that precise moment. For a moment I had abandoned who I was, what surrounded me, to live in that dream and believe I could make it come true. But then I thought of Anna in bed with Lorenzo, of Mery who would soon open the door of her house for me, unaware of what I had wanted that night, and I felt disgusted with myself.

"Nothing... I wouldn't have done anything about it."

"Do you want to tell me what happened?"

"I dreamed of her." After all it was true, even if I had wanted it was still a dream.

"I don't think if I had had her number I would have given it to you, anyway", Alex said, putting the phone down on the kitchen, then handed me the cup of coffee.

"You have more wisdom than me." I took a sip I found too bitter.

"No, it's not a matter of wisdom, you have too much noise in your head. You are about to get married and you're thinking about another woman, you're lying to your girlfriend, you're moving forward with your plans but it is evident you don't know if that's what you want."

"But how can I not want it?"

"I don't know, but what's certain is that you have to shed some light. You can't go on like this anymore hoping that fate, or time or God knows what will make things right for you. Miky, life is now, you have to decide to take it in your hands."

I looked down at the floor searching for an answer among the dark veins of the white marble. I felt stupid once again. Alex was right and I had known it for a long time, my life had been a succession of circumstances, of opportunities that I had undoubtedly been able to seize, but which I had not created for myself. I had never changed my path to discover new scenarios, different from those that had always been described to me. I had only fought for one thing in life against everything and everyone: the house in Barcelona. And I felt that was my most important achievement, but that was not it. It was as if after being able to make that dream come true I started seeing things from another point of view, wondering if the life I was leading was really mine or a reflection of the expectations of others.

I finished my coffee and grabbed the backpack containing my weekend clothes, then went back to the kitchen to say goodbye and got in the car to drive to Mery's house.

After a few hundred meters, she called me. She asked me to bring her the magazines she had left for me with the notes on the honeymoon. That weekend we would have finalized a choice.

I turned in the direction of my house trying to visualize them mentally somewhere inside the apartment, hoping not to have them stacked in an unreachable corner due to the construction site.

I went in, the dust in the room was thick as a fog bank and I lifted the collar of my shirt to cover my nose. I went straight to the places where I had imagined the magazines could be found and, discarding the first, I found them in the second. I took them on the fly without checking that they were all there, it had been such a long time I would not have remembered anyway, I put them in my backpack and left.

Arriving at Mery's house, almost an hour later, I found her on the phone with the wedding planner and instinctively rolled my eyes. I thought it was absurd to have to hire a professional to set up the church or set the table. I knew many couples who had done this on their own and had enjoyed it, but when I told Mery she looked at me as if I was asking her if I could wear a kilt at the wedding, so I threw my hands up and left her in full charge.

"Is everything going according to plan?" I asked her when she finished the call.

"All perfectly according to plan, except for the honeymoon and..." she left the sentence hanging as if to suggest that there was more, something I did not yet know but would soon be revealed to me.

"...And?" I urged her.

"I have some news."

I did not immediately understand the reason but

I had the impression that my heart had stopped. I looked at her, holding my breath as if preparing myself for a hard blow.

"Good or bad?" I asked stupidly, as her happy expression displayed the nature of the news I was afraid to hear.

"Do you remember the interview I had ten days ago?"

I exhaled, feeling liberated. Mery had been looking for an office in Perugia for some time to hire her, to be able to move without having to commute between home and work. Her last interview, she had told me, had been gone brilliantly.

"Of course, the office near the economics faculty."

By the way.

"Exactly! They called me yesterday, they liked me and they want to see me to make me a salary proposal and talk about schedules."

Although that news had immediately given me relief, I realized that it did not give me any joy, which I could instead read on my girlfriend's expression.

"Hopefully in a few weeks I'll be able to move in with you!"

"Sure but where? The house is not ready."

"What's that got to do with it? I'll wait for it to be." She looked at me tilting her head, as if she had only just now realized that I wasn't taking part in her euphoria.

"I was expecting you to be more excited."

I shook my head as if to wake up from a spell. "I'm sorry, you're right. This is great news. We have to celebrate," I recovered.

"It's early to celebrate, if they offer me a starvation wage I'll leave then and there. I honestly don't think so though, it's a great office and I'm pretty flattered

they chose me."
"And you are right to be."

We didn't have any big plans for that weekend. As always, the most exciting activity in that area was hiking the nearby hills which we would have done the following day, after lunch with the future in-laws. After I finished clearing the table, Mery suggested that I take a look at the magazines I had brought. I took them from my backpack and joined her on the couch.

"I'll make some tea", she said as I held the brochure of a five-star luxury resort, on which Mery had circled the image of the overwater room, with private access to the sea and a jacuzzi in the bathroom.

"What island is this?" I asked, raising my voice so that she could hear me from the kitchen.

"Ari Atoll... Maldives", she yelled over the kettle whistling. I realized I had an expression she would disapprove of. It's not that I didn't like the idea of sunbathing on a beach as white as baby powder with no thoughts other than relaxing, but I would have liked to spend those weeks better. After all, the opportunity of having longer holidays did not happen often. I leafed through the other proposals that ranged from the islands of French Polynesia to the Caribbean Sea, to the Indian Ocean including Seychelles and Mauritius. All beautiful places but my thought process was the same. I saw a block of printed sheets next to the catalogs stacked on the coffee table and I took it. They were the Mery's online searches and they outlined destinations that I found more fascinating. All countries located East, I read Thailand with a tour of the lands of the golden triangle and a few nights in Bangkok, Japan, Vietnam. I paused to read the articles and, with how those destinations were described, I marveled at the overwhelming desire to visit them all. The photos were also enchanting, albeit printed on regular paper: they were so deep they seemed three-dimensional. Some showed landscapes, others the faces of indigenous people and it was as if they were talking to me.

Suddenly I felt short of breath and a pain in my stomach made my abdomen contract. There was an inscription in the lower right corner of the photos I was looking at, and my gaze fell on it. On a loop, my mental voice kept reading the name written in italics. *"Anna Salemi Photography"*.

25

Mery went back into the living room and I instinctively put the papers on the coffee table in front of the sofa.

"What happened? You look distraught."

"Nothing, I was looking at the options." I tried to contain my agitation by masking it with an unnatural smile. I saw her approach with the glasses in which the ice cubes were rattling and, placing them next to those papers, picked them up. My heart was pounding in my chest like a drum.

"What shocked you so much about these articles?"

"How can articles upset me? Nothing, as I told you I was just taking a look." Trying to divert the conversation, I asked her what destinations she was most enticed by. She didn't seem convinced but sat down next to me and flipping through the printed pages, pulled an article about Bali from the pile.

"I want to relax, to look at the sea sitting on the beach. I know that the first three days would be nice for you, then you would start buzzing with boredom. So I abandoned the idea of locking ourselves up on an atoll and researched destinations that both of us could enjoy. Bali seemed the best to me."

I took the printed offer and, first of all, I looked at the photo: there was no digital signature and I thought it did not come from the same site. Better that way, I told myself.

I was still upset to have read that name, maybe it wasn't even her but at the very thought my legs had resumed a kind of frenzy that prevented me from holding them still and I placed my hand on my shaky knee. The temptation to pick up the computer and research *Anna Salemi Photography* was overwhelming, but I knew I had to wait until I was alone.

"Okay", I told her, "I'd say I might like it."

"However, I was thinking of having other estimates made by the travel agency, Thailand or perhaps an India and Maldives combo. What do you say?"

"Let's avoid the last one, you would never come to India anyway, better to keep Thailand and Bali as options."

"Perfect, I'm sending the agency an e-mail to get the quotes."

Mery got up from the couch to sit at her desk. As I heard the ticking of her fingers on the keyboard, my memory went back to that afternoon when, sitting at a table in the bar, Anna had told me about her job and her trips. I wondered if she had been in Bali and, for a very brief moment, I was tempted to look for her and ask her. It could have been useful for choosing the honeymoon. I shook my head amazed by the absurdity of that thought, but the curiosity to look her up increased with each passing minute. Who knows why I hadn't thought of it before. Maybe because I was trying not to shatter my life and that of my girlfriend.

"How's the suit search going?" It took Mery to curb those thoughts.

"What suit?"

"The wedding suit... or are you planning to get married in jeans and a T-shirt?"

"Indeed, I considered it."

The ensuing silence forced me to turn my gaze to her, who was staring at me seriously. "I mean, not in jeans and a T-shirt, of course. I was thinking of a spezzato, trousers and a shirt, something like that."

"Something like that? I mean, are you telling me you're going to open your closet and take a look at what you can wear on your wedding day?"

"If you put it that way, it seems there's something wrong with it. Anyway, I didn't say that."

I saw Mery's face light up in different shades of red starting to resemble the color of the fire. I kept the fixed and impassive gaze of someone who is absolutely certain not to be in the wrong.

"I wonder why I am wasting time organizing everything down to the smallest detail! I'm losing my mind to decide whether roses or tulips are better, the color of the sugared almonds, linen or silk tablecloths, updo or hair down, music, favors… and you? Haven't you even deigned to think that you might wear a suit at your wedding?"

"Look, I don't want you to take it that way. First of all, I have never asked you to worry about all these things, on the contrary, it seems to me that we are paying a professional wanted precisely by you so as not to have you subject yourself to this kind of stress.

Plus, you know I would be uncomfortable with a pinstripe suit."

She violently closed the laptop screen and I felt a pang of pain for it, then rising to her feet she put both hands on the desk and, in a high pitch, almost on the verge of screaming, she exploded: "I will be crushed inside a corset made of boning that will barely allow me to breathe and you... don't want to be uncomfortable? " She lowered her head, and when she raised it, I saw that she had tears in her eyes. "So it's true, you really don't give a damn about this wedding."

Seeing her in that state made me realize how insensitive I had been, I wished I hadn't but it was clear that the commitment and dedication she had invested in our big day were not in the least comparable to what I had, or rather that I hadn't, done myself. I felt mortified, walked over to her and hugged her.

"I'm sorry, you're right, I'm a fool." I kissed her hair and, stroking her back, tried to calm the sobs I had caused her. "It's not like that, you know, it's not true that I don't care. In fact, do you know what I'm going to do? I'll make an appointment today and go try on a few suits this week. Is that okay?"

She nodded her head in approval. "I just want everything to be perfect," she said with a sniff.

"And it will be." As I said those words, I felt a strange feeling of discomfort, as if my body had detected a dissonance between what I had said and what he perceived as real.

That afternoon I tried to look as interested in all the wedding preparations as possible, I listened to her listing the decisions made with the wedding planner regarding the flowers, church set-up, lunch menu, wedding favors and centerpieces; while on her dress there was an aura of mystery that Mery kept as the most important of secrets. I saw the spark ignite in her eyes and it was clear to me how much she had wished for my more active participation in the event. I added that new awareness to the list of things to feel guilty about. As I promised, I went to my room to pick up the phone and set up an appointment at a wedding suits store, but the reality was that I had no idea which shops to call.

"Hi, Al! Listen, I need a favor, I screwed up," I said in one breath to my friend who had answered the call.

"Suddenly I find myself with two children! What have you done this time?"

"I made Mery cry."

"Oh my God... what did you tell her?"

"That I was going to get married in jeans and a T-shirt."

A loud laugh came from the other side of the phone. "You're such a jerk!"

"I don't think you're allowed to talk like that."

"Why? Is a jerk a dirty word?"

"I don't know, ask Adele. Anyway, I made it right, but now I need your help. Could you make an appointment at the Cerchiari store? A friend of yours works there, if I remember correctly."

"Do you want to buy your wedding suit where I bought mine?"

"Yup."

"Ah well, a good omen"

"Come on, cut the bullshit, pick a good day for you. Because you will obviously come with me."

"Of course. Okay, I'll call them and keep you posted. However, know that, if things go wrong, the divorce will always cost you less than the dress."

"Heartwarming."

ne on, idiot, try not to do any more damage. 'l have twenty-four hours left there, you can

...ving settled the suit issue and waiting for a honeymoon quote, we could dedicate the rest of the weekend to doing nothing.

In the evening in bed, when the lamps were already out and only the glow of the moon illuminated the room, I felt stroking on my bicep, while Mery's mouth slowly approached my ear and nibbled my earlobe. I turned to her, ran my hand over her hips, leaning towards her lips to kiss her. At the exact moment our mouths made contact, a quick sequence of images made me revisit the love scene I had experienced with Anna, in that daydream. I let go abruptly sitting on the bed out of breath.

"What happened?" Mery asked in a bewildered tone.

"I don't know, I can't breathe well."

I kept taking in air, but it never seemed to reach my lungs. My hands were cold, sweaty, and as if anesthetized they did not respond to commands. I felt the rush of vomiting but it passed instantly and, with another breath, I tried to let oxygen in, then let out the air with a loud scream that came from the pit of my stomach and, with no control over my nerves, I let that monster of anguish, fear, guilt and anger out.

I kept shaking while Mery, not knowing what was going on, turned on the light and sat next to me stroking my back and asking me to talk to her.

"Miky, what's going on? You're make me worried so, explain..."

I could not do it, if I had spoken, if I had told her what I had hardly been able to hold back, then it would all be over. I wasn't ready to take that much risk.

"I don't know, I'm very tense," I said as soon as was able to relax my nerves.

Lowering her head she whispered: "I know, I see."

"I'm sorry, I didn't want to worry you"

"Miky, you have been worrying me for weeks, this is not the first time you have behaved strangely. Certainly never so evidently as tonight, but you have shown signs of discomfort other times recently."

Wow, just when I thought I was able to leave everything behind, to resume our usual life, our relationship as it was before everything changed on that trip to Barcelona. Still, Mery was telling me that it wasn't like that, that she realized that something had changed. "Is there something wrong with me? Don't you like me anymore?"

"Oh God no! Did I really make you believe this?" I felt so guilty I couldn't even hold her gaze. But I tried to, I made an effort to look into her eyes, it was difficult but I owed it to her.

"How long has it been, Miky, since we made love?"

"I don't know... maybe we have neglected too much in the last month what with the commitments of the house and the wedding."

"It's not just that, the few times it happened I felt you were distant." She lowered her eyes and added: "...and I'm afraid I know why."

A shiver of terror ran down my spine. "What do you mean?" I asked, anxiously awaiting her answer.

"I don't want to draw conclusions so I'm asking you... is it marriage that scares you and is pulling you away from me?"

It was time to confess everything, or at least part of it, what I would have to tell her sooner or later. I had decided to erase Anna from my life, I had chosen to

n way with Mery, so it didn't make sense
ut her, but I had the possibility to confess
t I had bought the house in Barcelona.
eing myself from that burden would have
ny conscience and, at the same time, would
have given her an explanation for the strange attitude she had noticed in me recently.

Mery was there, sitting cross-legged on the bed, her eyes full of anguish as she waited for my answer to free her from the doubt that gripped her.

"It wasn't my intention to create a distance, but maybe it's true, marriage scares me."

"I understand." She smiled and took my hand. "But we will take one step at a time, together, we will help each other deal with fear. We still have time to get used to the idea, you'll see, we'll be ready when get there."

Although I understood that a more favorable opportunity to clear my conscience would no longer happen, I was not able to. I held her tight, understanding the great love I felt for her.

The next day, as Mery seemed calmer after our conversation, I was pervaded by a deep sense of anguish. I kept wondering what the hell was wrong with me. Because I was no longer able to be happy, neither with Mery nor alone. It was as if with every step I took in one direction, something inside me was pulling me from another, sending out warning signs. I knew where I had decided to go, and I was going there. But part of me wasn't following me.

26

It was twenty past eight on Thursday morning and I was making coffee while I waited for my friends who would arrive any minute.

The house looked different now that the scaffolding had been removed and all that was left was cellophane on the furniture and on the floor. The bulk of the work had been done and Alex and Federica offered to help paint the walls. The first one arrived sleepily, but no trace of the second.

"I can't believe it's going to get even more beautiful than I designed it," Alex said, setting the paint cans and tools down on the floor. Federica was late and we started without her. Each of us had chosen a wall to paint and I thought it was fortunate that the tallest one had been knocked down.

"When will they set up the kitchen?" asked Alex who was working on the wall opposite mine.

"Next week."

"And then will Mery move in?"

The second interview had gone as she hoped and she would soon be resigning from her current employers.

I didn't answer Alex's question thinking about how much things would change in a matter of weeks. The wedding was approaching, but what immediately pressured me was the idea that Mery was leaving her old life to dive into the new one with me.

After finding Anna's name written on the photos, I searched for information on her. I hadn't found her on any social media, but I had tracked down the name of the magazine she worked for. I had browsed through all the articles published looking for her photos, picturing her wandering around those wonderful landscapes and I was not surprised I had found her such an interesting woman.

One evening, after reading about her latest published trip - Myanmar - I looked for the sweater I had left her after she had told me about that country.

I had worn it despite the heat, and although the numerous washes had taken away her scent, the image of when she had worn it was intact. Just like seeing on a photograph.

I had decided to face those doubts, to answer the questions that kept me awake at night and made me feel like everything I did was wrong.

How many times had I wondered what that kiss meant, how it could affect my feelings for Mery. I also found myself wondering why that day, before Mery told me about the interview, I had feared she was pregnant. Why was I petrified at the idea?

Understanding that Anna had caused an irreparable gash in my reality had been as difficult as admitting it.

Yet it was true, based on my understanding I had to make the decisions that would mark my destiny and that of Mery. I was getting there, but if it had been difficult to come out with it from the heart, putting it in words seemed impossible.

Meanwhile, time passed at a speed that seemed to have doubled and I knew that the moment to pump the brakes was now or never. The reason I hadn't done it yet was that I had no idea how to do it.

"Good morning, workmen," Federica shouted at the wide open door of the hall.

"About damn time," said Alex.

"I got donuts for breakfast."

"Donuts? Who likes donuts? Only you do!"

"Yes, and I bought them on purpose because I know they make you sick. Instead of complaining, you could say thank you! What did you bring? Let's hear it."

"The brushes. By the way yours is there, get to work."

Federica took a donut from the box and threw it at Alex fully hitting him on his bald head, he turned and, with his brush soaked in white paint, splashed her clothes making her curse. I watched that scene, grateful to have two friends like them, who with their mere presence were able to make me laugh and make me feel like I was in the right place.

After a few hours painting we stopped for lunch, we still had almost half of the house left, but by that evening we would have finished the job. The open windows allowed for air circulation to carry away the smell of fresh paint, letting in the scent of freshly cut grass. We waited for the pizzas we had ordered over the phone trying to get the white spots off our hands and, once they arrived, we sat on the floor in the center of the open space, ideally where the kitchen would be.

"Guys, I have to talk to you." I let those words out so I could not back down from doing it. Neither of them replied, but they began to listen.

"I don't know if I'm ready for the barrage of questions that will follow what I'm going to say but... I've decided to cancel the wedding."

"What?" Federica's shocked face justified her almost screaming. Alex, on the other hand, was staring at me with a serious expression, perhaps more serious than when he had told me about Giorgia. "Is it because of her? Because of Anna?"

"She was the thunderbolt that lit up the room. It brought light to everything I didn't want to see."

Being honest with myself had been the biggest challenge I had ever fought. I had listened to my heart scream its love for Anna and I had seen the wall of denial that my mind had built. My emotional side and rationality had fought to bring the truth to light: I couldn't marry Mery because deep down I didn't want to.

"Help us understand, Miky," Federica insisted.

"I would never do her any wrong. I know you think I have already and I could waste a lot of time trying to convince you otherwise, so now I want you to listen to what I'm going to say. I can't marry her. I cannot show up at the altar promising her something that I know is not authentic. In a few days she will quit her job, she will leave her house and her family behind to move here, and what would you say if I told you that I haven't even felt the teensiest bit of excitement about it?" I looked at Alex as if my words were meant solely for him. "I told myself that maybe I was scared, that my fear of change prevented me from enjoying it and then I wondered what I would feel if Anna knocked on my door with suitcases in hand ready to move in and I got excited just imagining it. I know it's not the same thing, that there's a world of difference between fantasy and reality, but now I know, I'm sure I want someone who happens not to be the woman who is about to move here. Right now, it would be more convenient to shut off my brain and take the path Mery and I have planned. It would be easier because deciding to leave her is deciding to kill her. I don't mean she can't live without me because I'm well aware she will, fortunately, but my Mery will die. I will never again be who I am now for her, and she will no longer be there for me." It was painful to even think about it, I felt a lump tighten my throat. "Letting go of her hand could also mean losing myself, I don't know, I never have before. I'm terrified. But the greatest gesture of love that I can do for her is not forcing her to live a great love, but not an endless one."

Struggling against a powerful feeling, I felt my eyes burn as they fought back tears. "How could I watch her walk towards me at the altar and know I lied to her?"

"Clearly", Federica said, taking my hand and squeezing it in hers. "But why are you going to leave her? Don't you think you could talk to her about your doubts, be honest about the house and see what happens? You could ask her to postpone the wedding for the time being."

"Fede, I can't go to Anna and tell her *'Please, let's wait, I have doubts about the wedding'*."

"To Mery."

"Yes... sure... to Mery."

Alex gave me a serious look after that slip of the

tongue and I stopped to observe the sincerity of my thoughts. Because I actually wanted to say those words to Anna.

"Don't wait a second longer," was all my friend told me.

27

I walked frantically in the apartment which, despite the packed boxes placed here and there in the rooms, had maintained a neat appearance. For the first time since Mery had given me the keys to her house, I felt like an intruder. Unable to sit and wait, I was washing the breakfast bowl my future ex-girlfriend had left in the sink earlier that morning on her way to work. I was hoping that Mery hadn't spoken to her managers about resigning yet, despite having confirmed that she would be doing so in the afternoon. I was afraid that, for some more favorable circumstance, she had found a way to tell them that morning.

Driving there, I had tried to build the speech I would tell her as soon as she returned for lunch. The timing was not the best, I told myself, but I couldn't wait until it was too late. The doorbell rang, making me jump. I went to the intercom and the female voice answering made me realize the time had come.

ne." I waited for her in front of the door I held th my hand as I listened to the sound of her , one after the other, and felt my heart beating with them. I let her in and asked her to take a seat in the living room, letting her walk ahead of me. She seemed lost and I figured she didn't understand why I'd summoned her there, at that strange hour, on that random day of the week. Without making small talk first, I took a seat opposite her. She chose the couch and I sat down on the coffee table so I could look her in the eyes. I took a deep breath, my hands clasped and sweaty, and looked her straight in the eye.

"I called you here for a very serious reason, your sister will be here in a few minutes so please let me speak and keep your comments and insults for later. As I said, Mery will be here shortly and I will tell her that..." I had to stop, trying to calm my anxiety over what I was about to say. "I'll tell her the marriage is canceled. I have decided to call and tell you first so that once I'm gone you're going to be here, already aware of the reason why she'll in that state. I wanted someone who would understand, without her having to relive everything."

She waited for me to speak on, perhaps to make sense of what she had heard.

"Are you kidding me? Please tell me you're kidding." Her shrill voice gave me a shiver that ran down my spine, I was prepared to receive her wrath, but I had deemed it necessary because once I spoke to Mery, I knew that I would be gone forever, and I would not be there, and I would not have been able to, knowing she was there alone.

"No, Vale, it's all true. I'm not interested in giving you explanations at the moment, I just want to tell Mery and know that you'll be with her later."

She looked at me bewildered, but I could di see her face blush and her anger, made ever by the way she had tightened her mout accentuating the hard line of her jaw.

"I'm going to kill you! Explanations? Do you think I want explanations? I want to put my hands on your neck, I want to blow your head off, I want to run you over my car and then put in reverse! Explanations? Explanations on what? That you're a son of a..."

"Mery, hi!" I spun around at the sound of her keys unlocking the front door.

"Hi baby, Vale, what are you doing here? What happened? Are you guys fighting?" Unprepared to find us there, she stood with her briefcase in her right hand and the set of keys in her left.

"No, Mery... Vale has just stopped by, now she's going to wait for us in the other room because I have to tell you something."

Valentina, getting up from the sofa to go and lock herself in the kitchen, gave me a look that made my blood run cold.

I asked Mery to sit in the seat her sister had left empty.

"Oh my God, what happened? Is it the dress? Did it break? Did they call you about it? Was it stained?"

"No, Mery the dress is fine, we're not here for the dress."

"The church?"

"No, not even the church."

"Then what? The priest is dead! He was old! What, Miky, what?"

"Mery... I understand that there is no other way to tell you, so I'll just come out and say it." I stopped to gather all the courage I thought I had and it suddenly evaporated from my body. "I want to cancel the wedding."

She remained motionless in front of me, white as a corpse, her mouth partially open at the end of the last words I had spoken, looking in my eyes for a sign that would make her understand that I was joking. But she knew it, she knew that I could never tease her that way, so she regained her strength and asked me: "'Cancel' meaning there's something, which I can't think about at the moment, preventing you from participating at our wedding in six weeks? Or 'cancel' meaning that... you're leaving me?" She sounded strong as she asked me, but then fear broke her voice. "Are you leaving me?"

Looking into her eyes, I nodded.

She jumped up as if she chose to escape, but only began to walk from one side of the room to the other, trying to tame her completely out of control breathing. She pressed her right hand to her chest, as if trying to keep her crazed heart still or keep it from shattering. She sat down in front of me and, picking up the pieces, asked me: "Why?"

"Because it's not enough to promise you it will be forever."

"I'm paralyzed, I can't feel anything anymore... I'm dead." She put her head in her hands and, after a long moment of silence, said: "It's not because of the wedding."

"I know it's not because of the wedding."

"No, really, I don't give a damn about the wedding. If you think we could be happy not getting married, if you think that's what you're scared of, let's cancel it. Let's cancel it together, we've been fine until today without getting married. I don't need it."

I wondered if that was true. "I've thought about this too, I've thought about it a lot. But I'm not afraid of marriage. I believe in marriage, which is why I can't do it. And I can't even stay with you if I'm not ready to marry you. I will never love you more than that and if it's not enough now, it will never be."

"It's enough for me."

I saw the effort in holding back the tears that perhaps out of pride, or perhaps out of fear of admitting that it was really happening, she had decided to tame. I wondered how the man I had been in the last few months was enough for her, the man who hadn't always been able to physically love her, the man who had left her alone to plan a wedding, the man who hadn't been able to get excited when she found a job in the city. The man who had hidden the purchase of a house from her and, even worse, the man who loved another woman. Sure, she didn't know that, but how could I have looked like a good husband? Perhaps, just like it happened to Alex, Mery also had a picture of me, of us, and it would take a while to understand that it did not correspond to reality.

"I've never imagined going through a moment like this, so I don't even know if I'm reacting in the right way. Maybe I should throw your stuff and everything I could find at you. I should tell you the worst things I can think of and maybe even spit in your face... but I can't. I can't get angry, I don't even want to cry. I can't feel anything but empty."

She got up again and went to the window, turned her back to me and put a hand against the glass that looked out over the flower garden. "I don't want to know any more, I don't want to know if there's someone else, so please, if there is, do me a favor and don't tell me." She rested her head on her arm which, from how slow the movement was, seemed very heavy.

Unable to add more, I stared at her slender figure in that statuesque pose realizing I had done it. I had let *my* Mery go.

"I don't want to know more," she repeated. "That's enough. Go away before I have the strength to react, please."

I got up slowly. "Alright. I'm not going say everything I'd like to, because I understand it's not appropriate now. But all I'm going to say is I have never wanted to cause you pain, not even a second of my life. Even if you don't give a shit. Understandably. Goodbye, Mery."

These last words were pushed out of my stomach with anger, disappointment, tears and a lot of pain. Much more than I imagined feeling. And it was a lot.

As soon as I closed the door behind me, I heard her burst into violent tears. I listened to Valentina run to her and I was happy I had called her, glad that she had someone ready to hold the hand I had just left.

28

The next few weeks went by between calls from friends and family asking why the wedding was canceled. Feeling overwhelmed by the amount of things I had to deal with, the wedding planner had taken on the burden of informing the guests of the change of plans, a "favor" that had cost me less than the sacrifice it would have been to do it myself. I had made sure at all costs that Mery was not to be involved in the wedding cancellation whatsoever, so I had been quite busy, between that and my job at university, I hadn't had time to stop and think about the future, or worse, the present.

Federica had helped me with the move a few days earlier: what was supposed to be our house was ready after the wedding, and I was leaving Alex's house to go back to living alone. During the drive she had asked me what I was going to do. I replied that

I would spend the month in the house in Barcelona, leaving, for a twist of fate, on the very day of the canceled wedding.

She was very surprised when, after asking me if I was going to look for Anna, I said no. I did not think I would, plus, as I had already reflected in the past, she had not reached out either. I was certain that she had chosen to fix things with her husband and save their marriage. If not even the secret he had kept from her was enough for her to take her wedding ring off, surely a kiss with a stranger in a moment of great emotional confusion, was not going to be an incentive. Obviously the meaning that kiss had held was different for each of us. I loved her, I was sure of that. Nothing I had done after meeting her would have ever been possible in the absence of that feeling. Maybe fate, God or the universe had sent her to me for that very reason: I was leading a life that was not the right one, neither for me nor for the people who were involved in it and she, with her arrival and her wonderful sweetness, had been the lightning that had woken me from my sleep. That was the point of meeting her.

I was sitting on the swivel stool at the kitchen counter looking around. The packed suitcases, full of everything I had decided to take to the Rambla de Catalunya house, were lined up next to the door. The light from the burning lamps was dim, an amber yellow that gave the room a welcoming warmth. I had not returned or replaced anything we had ordered to furnish this nest, so I found myself alone, looking at the house Mery and I had imagined in every detail. I unwillingly ate the pasta I had cooked for myself, shaking my head every time my brain realized that the next day I was due to get married. I wondered how I would have spent that evening if things had turned out differently. Would I have been out celebrating my last night of "freedom" with friends, or would I have found myself in the same position as now wondering what the hell I was doing? I would never know.

I thought about Mery, and wondered how she was getting by. I hadn't heard from her since the day I left her. There had been occasions that required a confrontation, but she had always delegated Valentina. Even when the travel agency called me to ask if I was planning to take the trip to Bali, it was the clerk who informed me that Mery had given up her half. Obviously, I was not going to leave for my honeymoon alone, and when the girl suggested I go with a friend, I told her to cancel my share as well and send the full refund to Mery.

While I was immersed in those reflections, an unexpected noise caught my attention, by instinct I got up from the stool brandishing my fork. The front door opened and what I saw paralyzed me in that attacking position, armed with cutlery. As soon as she became aware of my presence she stopped in front of the open door.

A moment of silence left the opportunity for both of us to say the first word, but the wall of tension that had materialized in the middle of the room seemed to keep us at a distance.

I didn't expect to see you here.
Why are you here?
Why... why... why am I brandishing a fork?
I lowered the weapon. "I think I won't need this."

The silence now broken, I took a step towards her and invited her in.

She walked slowly putting one foot in front of the other like someone balancing on a beam. She was staring at me and I smiled at her. It wasn't a casual smile, I was happy to see her.

"Sorry, I shouldn't have come."

"You did the right thing, actually."

She smiled too and the air seemed to become less dense, more breathable.

"I came to give you these." She put her hand on the counter, leaving the set of keys on it.

"Would you like something to drink? Are you hungry?"

"No, I'm fine, thanks."

Her face was tense but her features were as clean and regular as I remembered them. She seemed to have lost weight and I naively hoped that I wasn't the cause.

"How are you?" The question might seem trivial, but I needed to ask it. So many times since that day I had had the urge to pick up the phone and call her to find out how she was, but every time, every damn time, I knew it would just be selfish of me. I hated going from the one who helped her in difficult times to the one who had to stay away from her to prevent her from suffering.

"Fine" she replied.

I wanted to ask her why she chose that very night to come, the night before our failed wedding. Then I thought that maybe she had come for that reason, to let me know that she was "fine".

"Okay, maybe I should say something too," she whispered, straightening her back. "Of course I could have gotten you the keys in a thousand other ways but..." She looked around, turning her head in different directions. "I wanted to see it."

"The house?"

"Yup. I thought it might be my last chance."

"You did the right thing," I repeated.

"I'm really sorry, I don't know why but I was convinced you were still at Alex's."

"I've been here for about ten days." I turned to look at the apartment, accompanying the movement with my arm. "How does it look?"

"How we would have wanted it." She smiled with resignation.

I went to the refrigerator and took a bottle of wine, two glasses from the cupboard and placed them in front of her filling them.

She accepted that unspoken invitation to stay by grabbing the one closest to her and took a sip. "Are you leaving?" she asked pointing to the suitcases.

"Yes, tomorrow."

"Me too, where are you going?"

"You first, my answer's going to take some time."

She raised her eyebrows but then replied, "I'm going to Bali."

My eyes widened. "Damn, I think yours takes time too."

"Not so much, I decided to leave alone for our honeymoon. I wanted to go to Bali and couldn't find a valid reason not to."

"You're absolutely right."

"What about you?"

"I'm going to Barcelona."

She laughed. "What's new!"

"There is something new, actually." She looked at me and I knew I had caught her attention. "I bought the house."

Her eyes opened like the petals of a flower in spring and, beyond her amazement, I was moved to see a shy smile. She put down her glass and placed her hand on my thigh. The hairs on my arms stood up like antennae at her warm touch.

"Finally," she said.

I was relieved by that answer. I found no reason to tell her more about when it had happened.

"You know," she continued, lowering her gaze and looking up at me immediately after, "I've thought about this a lot since you left me." A blow to the stomach twisted me as I was punched without warning. "I think I have my share of responsibility."

I wanted to stop her but let her talk. "Once I supported your wish, do you remember when I used to tell you not to give me presents on Christmas or birthday because we would have shared the greatest gift together by buying the house?"

I nodded accepting the pain of those memories. "Sure."

"It was true, I really wanted it too. Then I don't know what happened but I understood when it happened. At some point, which was shortly after I turned thirty-five, life began to go at such a speed I felt like I couldn't get ahold of it. So I started to fear time, I started thinking that I hadn't had a baby yet and that the more time passed, the more chances a child wouldn't come. But you know how I see it, first I wanted to get married and that's when I started pushing for a wedding. Even the proposal... would you still have done it, if I hadn't pestered you for a whole year talking about marriage, living together, our future and starting a family every single day?"

I smiled as I remembered that period which had been exactly as she had just described it.

"Actually..."

"I know. It's just that when I entered that vortex I was dragged away by you, by us, by what we were before the race to make our love official made us mad.

I haven't been a good partner in the last few years and you haven't been in the last few months, but I didn't want to see it." She held the glass of wine and it looked like she wanted to fill a great void with the sip she took.

"I'm glad you're here tonight."

"Tonight…" She sighed.

"How are your parents? I thought a lot about them too. I feel bad for never saying goodbye to them, for never talking about all this with them. They welcomed me like a son and I miss them, but I don't know if they would like to see me."

"Not now, maybe in a while."

"Of course."

"On the other hand, it's better if you don't see Vale, actually, if you haven't already, I suggest you get your car insured against vandalism."

I laughed. "I'll take care of it."

"Thank you for asking her to come over that day."

"It was the least I could do."

"Thanks anyway." She got up and took another look at the house.

"Do you want to look around?" I asked.

"No, thanks, that's enough for me." She picked up the purse she had hooked to the stool. "Good luck," she said, looking at me without resentment.

"Good luck to you too."

With my damp robe on and my wet hair, I was running the brush full of shaving cream across my face. I had been using the one that once belonged to my father for years, however I had recently had the darker straw-colored bristles on top replaced. The handle, on the other hand, was always the same, made of dark wood with an inscription indicating the brand that was almost completely faded. My mother had given it to me on a day of excessive melancholy, telling me it was too painful to see it on the bathroom shelf every morning. "I'll be happier if you take it, at least you know how to use it", she told me.

The previous night had not been an easy one, in an alternation of being asleep and awake. With each movement, from the moment I put my feet down, I kept wondering if I would have chosen the same gestures in preparation for the ceremony. Instead I was getting ready for the trip and, despite some enthusiasm, my mood was shaken by Mery's visit the night before.

I had been really happy to see her, perhaps more than ever considering the particular evening, but greeting her and looking at her back as she walked out the door had been difficult and painful. I already knew that I would miss having her in my life, but only then did I fully realize it.

As the blade cut through the stiff hairs of a three or four day beard, the doorbell rang. I checked the time on my cell phone and it seemed too early for Alex to roll up. We agreed that he would stop by at ten o'clock to take me to the airport, two hours before my departure for Barcelona. It was half past eight.

"Hello?"

"It's me."

"Already? I'm still shaving."

"I'm coming up, have you already had breakfast?"

"No."

"Then I'll get two croissants down here at the bar and bring them over."

I pressed the button to open the gate and door and went back to the mirror to finish shaving.

A few minutes later Alex came in carrying breakfast.

"Why are you already here?"

"I took Adele to Giorgia's and by now I was out and about."

"How are things with her?"

"Good with Adele." He smiled and quickly changed the subject. "So... how are you feeling? Is it strange to think that you were supposed to get married today?"

"Pretty strange."

"Any regrets?"

"No, I'm just a little disheartened." I took a bite of the croissant. "I saw Mery last night."

I knew I was launching an unexpected missile and indeed Alex stared at me for a moment before asking me for more details. I told him about her impromptu visit and the words we had exchanged. I told him that, although it hadn't been easy, her visit had relieved me of a burden.

"You are two very smart people, you have taken the opportunity to end your relationship in a dignified manner."

"She's the smart one, I never would have had the balls to do it."

As I spoke, Alex shifted in his chair as if he were leaning against a back of poison oak. "Aren't you going to dry your hair?" he asked me.

"Not from May to September."

"Won't your neck hurt?"

I frowned. "Why should it?"

"My grandfather always told me that if I left with wet hair my neck would hurt afterwards."

"Instead, something worse happened."

He got up and reached into his pocket and pulled out a folded piece of paper. "Here", he said, dropping it on the kitchen counter.

"What's that?"

"Your wedding present."

I winced and opened it. "What's that?" I repeated stupidly.

"Her phone number."

I stared at him without blinking, holding the note open with both hands. "How did you do it?"

"I've always had it."

I was serious and maybe angry, Alex rushed to explain. "The night we got back from Barcelona I was on the couch talking on the phone. When I hung up, I looked at the calls and saw the one you made from Anna's number. On the plane you told me you fell in love with her, so I saved it."

"I'm not going to call her."

"I know."

"Then why are you giving it to me?"

"Because now I can."

"Explain, please."

"Last time, when you asked for it, when you woke me up because you dreamed of her and you were hoping it was still saved in my incoming calls, remember?" I nodded. "At first I wasn't sure and that's why I asked you what you wanted to do with it. You were totally freaking out and you had no idea. Then, with your feet on the ground, you realized that you could not use it and I agreed. You had to make things right with Mery and get some clarity. Now you got some and I think it's the right moment for you to have it."

"Today, as I did then, I'm telling you I can't use it."

"That's not true. Last time you couldn't, now you don't want to. There's a difference."

"She's married."

"You don't know that."

"Yes I do!" I raised my voice unwittingly. "And you

do too."

"Things have changed for you and they may have changed for her too. Have you ever thought that maybe she hasn't looked for you for the same reason you haven't? She knows you're getting married today. Even if she had left her husband, do you really think she would have come to you and threatened to screw it up?"

I swallowed a mouthful of saliva and felt my Adam's apple move first up then down. Did I think about it? Sure. But by then the situation was stuck in a vicious circle. I could not look for her, risking to disrupt a couple's balance that perhaps they had struggled to find again, and maybe she had not done so for the same reason. In any case, I would have never known.

"Why don't you call Lisa? You can ask her and ask that she doesn't tell Anna."

"Yeah, right, would you do it?"

"What?"

"Hiding Anna calling you about me from me."

He looked up before answering. "No, not now."

"Would you have before?"

"Well, if that had been the case... while you were with Mery ... knowing it would upset you ... No, I couldn't have hidden from you."

I leaned against the kitchen counter. "I swear that for a moment I thought I was going to punch you in the face."

"Can't you see how much you care about her?"

I nodded. "Yup. It's one of the few things I'm certain of."

"Exactly... and another one is that if we don't leave now, you'll miss your flight."

"Right."

29

Entering that house caused much stronger emotions than the first time, in several respects.

The first, the house was now mine. The second, it was no longer a disaster like last time: the team of workers I had called had already restored the plaster and painted the walls white, and they were now perfect. But the turning point was given by the floor: after being cleaned and polished, it had regained its marvelous shades of light blue, blue, teal and yellow that lit up in the sunlight bringing a real kaleidoscope of colors into the house.

The third was Anna. The last time I had been in there was with her and nothing had been the same ever since. When I opened the window and went out onto the terrace, my heart was struck by a series of blows, one stronger than the other.

In the first few days, I made many trips to several

stores to buy basic furniture. First of all, the bed. I had already had the new bathroom fixtures assembled, but the cabinet and tub were missing. At the time I was using the outdoor shower, the one I had put on the terrace to enjoy the jet of water under the blue of that clear summer sky. I had confirmed the kitchen design that they would set up as soon as I finished working on the wall.

In fact, what was left to do was just to tear down the wall that divided the kitchenette from the living room. My idea was to have an open kitchen with an island to eat on and separate the two rooms with a wooden table. Ideally the layout became similar to that of my old apartment, but the materials and colors I had chosen made this a much more lively and... Spanish house. For the moment I was content with cooking on the barbecue using the gas stove for different uses. Living there again was incredible. I would get up early in the morning without needing an alarm and full of energy, ready for a new day of dedicating myself to the renovation and strolling through those streets, no longer as a tourist but as a local, even if partially.

I felt a rush of pride when I wrote my name on the doorbell. Miguel Mancini.

In the evening I would set up the camping table outside, turn on the string of outdoor lights I had bought at Ikea, sit on the deck chair and, a cold beer in hand, imagine moving there permanently. I would have needed a career change, first of all, but more than that, the idea of distancing myself from Alex and Federica, my only family, held me back from actually doing it. Sometimes I would take the note with Anna's number and turn it over in my hands. Would I ever call her? Maybe. Then I looked at the wall on which I was leaning before kissing her: another corner of the terrace that now housed my memories.

All in all I was happy.

The late August sun was incredibly hot and made the outdoor floor impractical. I had bought one of those giant garden umbrellas to protect myself from the heat during the day. Peppers of various colors, zucchini and a steak were arranged on the barbecue, beginning to give off an exquisite scent.

I heard the phone ring but reached for it too late.

The number was unsaved, it was a landline with an area code that I was not familiar with.

It was Sunday and I didn't know who could be looking for me from who knows where in Italy.

I called the number back.

"Hello?" A male voice.

"Yes, hello, I'm Michele. Michele Mancini. I found your call."

"Miky, hi, I'm Paolo."

"Paolo?"

"Paolo Sirti."

"Paolo, hi! What number is this?"

"Sorry, I called you from my landline. Wait a second, I'll be right there, stay on the line…" While waiting I tried to think of some reason why Paolo Sirti would look for me.

We were friends, yes, but not that close, we just saw each other a couple of times a year for a beer in honor of our university days. He lived in Veneto but I didn't remember where exactly, and the last time we saw each other he had recently married. It had been a few days before Christmas, he was in Perugia to spend the holidays with his family and we had gotten a classic Christmas happy hour drink with our university mates. Not all of them, just the nice ones. The quick review of the information I had on him had yielded no results.

"Here I am."

"Here you are."

"First of all, sorry to bother you on a Sunday."

"No problem."

"How is Mery?"

"She's in Bali on our honeymoon." Silence. "We broke up before the wedding and she left alone. Let's pretend you're not too surprised, shall we?"

"Perfect. Just to be polite... are you okay?"

"Wonderful."

"Great. I called to make you an offer Listen..."

"I'm listening."

"You know I have a training agency, right?"

"Yup."

"Great. Do you know that we offer professional courses to people who want to become entrepreneurs?"

"Mhmm... more or less."

"Okay. We'll hold a two-day course in September and I would like to ask you to join us and be a speaker on the first day."

"Speaker for what?"

"Economics."

"What would I do?"

"Nothing different from what you do in the classroom with your students. The topics are: asset management, reports, annual budgets, business plans... anyway, I will send you the program if you're interested. Oh, you would obviously be compensated for your time."

"I don't know, Paolo, I've never done such a thing. I don't think I'm the right person for the job."

"But you do it every day at university. Don't think

it's different. Indeed, often the people who come to the courses have no experience in economics or marketing so you should talk about the basics. Come on, you've always been one of the best, don't tell me no."

"When would it be?"

"The twelfth of September. It's a Saturday in the afternoon. In Verona."

"Verona?"

"Yes, should I send you the program?"

"Send it. How long until you need an answer?"

"As soon as possible. The course has been planned for some time, but a speaker blew us off so I just need someone to fill in for that day. If you say no, I'll have to start looking again."

"Okay, I'll give you an answer by tomorrow."

"Thanks, Miky, talk to you tomorrow. I'll send you the e-mail."

During lunch I took a look at the program that Paolo had attached to the e-mail, whose text was only: *"I'm counting on you"* with three exclamation points.

Indeed, the talking points were absolutely familiar to me and it would have been no problem presenting them in front of an audience, one without any experience no less. I checked my calendar. By that time I would have had to return to work at university anyway, so the commitment would not have forced me to cut my vacation short. I put down the computer and relaxed on the deck chair with my hands behind my head and my legs crossed.

Why not? I told myself. It could have been an opportunity to try something different in my profession. Since I had graduated, apart from some training and barely paid internships, I had done nothing but teaching. Well, sure, that assignment would have required me to play the same role, but the idea of speaking to people who would immediately apply my notions gave me the impression that it would be a more interactive and dynamic experience. Besides, I had never been to Verona. I decided to think about it for a while longer, taking advantage of the time I had taken to do so.

I looked at that terrace. I loved it and I loved being there. It made me feel at home like no other place in the world. It had been hard to get there but all the suffering and the burning desire I had felt for that place made that moment, that achievement, even more special. I looked at the far right corner hoping to see my mother painting again, but this time it didn't happen. I made up my mind.

I got up and left the house. After a couple of hours, I returned with what I had purchased. I opened it and started assembling the pieces. Once I had finished, I went out onto the terrace and put the easel there, where it had always been. I entered the house and reached for the only suitcase I had not yet emptied, in which I had put three paintings, all made by my mother. Only one of the three, who was just a little younger than me, had been painted before she moved to Italy. I had seen it hanging on the kitchen wall at my parents' house for years, I remembered my mother looking at it as if it were a window into her past life. It depicted the view from the terrace, with the columns of the Sagrada Familia and the usual sky of an intense blue sprinkled with white clouds. I put it on the easel. It looked like a postcard, a miniature of reality. I looked at it and at that space in its entirety. It was perfect.

In the evening, after returning from a tour of the city followed by a seafood dinner on the beach, I got into bed with my laptop on my lap to check out flights. Upon departure I had only purchased a one way ticket because I had no idea how long I would have stayed, or if the remodel would have required me to be there longer. In fact there the kitchen wall was still to fixed and I would have liked to resolved the matter before returning to Italy.

I decided that I would call the company the following day and, based on the agreements made with the builders, I would book the flight.

I felt a bit of disappointment when I saw that there was a direct flight from Barcelona to Verona. I had toyed with the idea of having to land in Milan, perhaps in search of a sign that would lead me to believe that it was right to look for Anna. But then, estimating how long the train route from Milan to Verona would be on Google Maps, I realized that yes, it could be done, but it would have been a stretch, certainly not fate.

The next day I put my plan into action by calling the construction company early in the morning. The supervisor told me that they wouldn't have been able to work on my apartment before mid-September. I resigned myself to the idea of not completing the renovation before returning to Italy, thinking that I would have to spend a few weekends there in the following month. It wasn't a big deal, since I didn't have any other commitments.

I sent a message to Paolo accepting his offer and when he sent me the detailed outline of the topics that I would have dealt with, I got to work to prepare my presentation.

Two weeks later, after closing all the windows and turning off the boiler, I was ready to leave my new, old home again. This time I did it with a light heart, knowing that I would be back soon and that I would not have to find excuses to do so. I double-locked the door and, with a much lighter luggage than the one I had when I flew in, I took a taxi, which was waiting for me a few meters from my house, to the airport.

As soon as I got out of the plane I felt the humid heat of the Po valley. The journey from the airport to the center of Verona was short and not particularly scenic. Instead, I was amazed by the beauty of the center when the taxi dropped me a few steps from the hotel.

My lecture was set for that afternoon and I had some free time to take a tour of the city. I went to my room to leave my suitcase, I sent a message to Paolo to let him know of my arrival, and he gave me an appointment in his office an hour before the start of the course.

30

I checked out the path I would have to take to get to the conference; discovering that it was in the center, I walked out of the hotel.

Among the various places that I would have liked to visit that weekend were Piazza delle Erbe, Juliet's house and, of course, the Arena. *Mundanely touristy*, I told myself, but I couldn't have left without seeing them. I made a quick mental count of the time I had available and headed for the first chosen stop. After a spectacular view from the top of the Lamberti tower, I sat down at a coffee table spellbound by the timeless beauty of Piazza delle Erbe. Reaching the square I had witnessed the exit of two spouses from the Palazzo della Regione. I had stopped to observe a moment that seemed to represent the end of many children's fairy tales: white flowers and tulle adorned the stairs, while the bride smiled at the cameras and seemed to shine with her own light. A horse-drawn carriage awaited the newlyweds at the end of the human corridor of guests. Although I found that excessive, I had picked up the phone and taken a photograph. After making sure I had fully captured the bride and especially the dress, I sent it to Alex with the caption *"For Adele"*.

Wedding dresses were her great passion. Those images made me think of Mery and, more than remorse, I continued to feel sorry for having disappointed her. I imagined how she would feel if she were the one who got confronted with that scene and it broke my heart. I thought of her in Bali, even though she must have been back by now, but I liked to imagine her there enjoying the serenity of that island.

Sitting at the table I observed the people around me. The square was packed with people of different nationalities. I could hear English, Spanish, French, Russian and, inevitably, Chinese.

It was easy to recognize the locals. They were the only people who did not notice the beauty that surrounded them. I looked at the time on my cell phone: it was a quarter past three and I set out on the road.

Paolo greeted me at the entrance and then took me to his office. He invited me to put my stuff on a desk, then offered me a coffee. "Did you have a good journey?" he asked me.

"Pretty quiet, thanks."

Although we had known each other for decades, in that particular situation there was a slight disconnection, rather common between employer and professional in training. He showed me where the course was going to be held: it was a real conference room, complete with a small stage with a speaker station, including a microphone and a white cloth behind it for the projection of images, about fifty chairs arranged in rows of ten and a neon light also typical of university classrooms. A buffet table was set up in the corridor with pretzels, pizzas, canapés, fruit and soft drinks.

"We're saving the prosecco for the end, because we want them to be awake during the course" chuckled Paolo at the end of the tour.

He gave me a name tag which I hooked to my shirt pocket.

People began to arrive, crowding into the corridor and attacking the buffet table. I went to my temporary study to arrange the material and look at the setlist, mentally repeating the topics. I was supposed to entertain the audience for about an hour and a half, then devote the next half hour to questions. I took my wallet out of my trouser pocket but, before putting it in my backpack, I opened it by pulling out the paper containing Anna's number. I reread it for the millionth time, it was a catchy number sequence. Five months had gone by, and yet thinking about her was still the most beautiful thing I could do. The desire to smile, keep fit, enjoy my time, read a book and drink a glass of wine, to look at the blue sky and feel happy at the very thought that she existed came back to me. A tiny possibility that life would sooner or later put us back on the same path was what made me look to the future with hope and optimism. Yet I was not ready to look for her. Something, when I looked at that number, kept me from fantasizing about a possible future together. It was the fear that it might never happen, that the things we wanted weren't the same. The possibility that we loved each other from a distance in the secret of our silences was more comforting than the fear of finding out my love was not reciprocated.

I folded the paper and put it in my pocket.

The corridor, meanwhile, had become a too crowded backroom in which I slowly advanced, avoiding rash movements, to refrain from hitting people and their glasses. I saw Paolo waving to me to join him. He introduced me to a number of people whose names I no longer remembered while they were still talking to me when, out of the corner of my eye, I thought I saw something. I turned abruptly. There were only heads, a flood of heads of different colors, among which there was none that I was familiar with. Still, sure I hadn't hallucinated, I stood on my tiptoes to look at the crowd better. It was obvious that my mind was still playing tricks on me.

It was when Paolo invited me to have something to drink that, turning to face the table, I saw her.

As if the room had suddenly fallen silent, I could only hear the sound of my heart. The people around us had become indefinite shapes, a palette of nuanced colors that stood out even more against the sharpness of the image before my eyes. She was standing there, a few meters from me, as beautiful as I remembered her, but not a fantasy this time... and she was staring at me with the same incredulous expression.

I raised my hand but I had the impression that gesture looked more like a boy scout greeting, so I immediately lowered it. She was still, looking like a statue. A beautiful statue. Paolo called my attention and I answered him without looking at him: "Excuse me... excuse me a moment." I took a few steps and, as I approached her, I listened to my heart restart, speed up... it made so much noise that I couldn't hear my thoughts. She walked towards me until she was in front of me.

I would have hugged her, squeezing her until she was out of breath, I would have caressed her like that

in front of her hotel, I would have taken her away
there, because now I didn't give a damn about
re I was, about my commitments. But I was silent
and just stood there. Until a burst of energy, perhaps
caused by my spirit of survival, made me react.
"Anna..."
"Hi."
I swallowed hard at the sound of her voice and
closed my eyes imperceptibly, as if to register it in my
mind.
"What are you doing here?" she spoke before me.
"I have to teach a course, I'm... the speaker."
"The business management course?" She had a
bewildered look and a trembling voice. I lost myself
in those magnificent green eyes. "The business
management course?" she repeated.
"Yes... sorry. Yes... that one."
"Your name wasn't on the schedule."
"I joined in at the last minute." What were we
talking about? After five months spent dreaming of
this meeting, the last thing I wanted to talk about was
the business management course. We had to leave, I
had to find a way to get her out of there. But how? I
didn't even know what she was came here for.
"Why are you here?" I asked her.
"For the course."
"Do you need it for your job?"
"It's a long story, I don't work for the magazine
anymore because it was... let's say shut down. I
started a company with the man who used to be my
boss, Angelo, and he wants me to be as prepared to
run the company as he is, so he signed me up for this
course and now... I'm here."
I got the impression that she was as excited as
I was. But then I told myself that maybe she was

embarrassed by what had happened between us and that she had probably done everything to erase it from her memory. That would have been a disaster.

Paolo gestured to an imaginary watch on his wrist urging me to begin. I didn't want to get away from her, but the thought of her being part of the audience increased my motivation. I imagined taking her to dinner after that engagement.

"I think you have to go," she whispered, staring at me with those eyes I never thought I'd see again. Not that day. Not there.

"Yes, I'm going, are you coming?"

"In a minute."

"Listen, don't run away at the end of the course, I'd like to..." *take you away* "... talk to you again."

"Yeah, sure."

I walked to the door of the conference room but after a few steps I stopped. With a gesture dictated by instinct or madness, I went back and approaching the skin of her face, I kissed her cheek.

"You don't know how happy I am to see you", I murmured in a low voice. She smiled at me, but she seemed more troubled than flattered, and I had the terrifying impression that it wasn't the same for her.

I began my lesson distracted, as well as by her presence, by the perception I had had shortly before. I could not believe she was there, it really was fate, I could have never imagined, thought or planned to find her in front of me in that place, at that moment, for that occasion. Yet she was there, and she was gorgeous. Although I tried to speak to the entire audience, my gaze always fell on her. I had to make a huge effort to keep my train of thought. With the stolen glances I managed to cast I saw her taking notes, get settled in her chair several times, looking for something in her bag, writing on her cell phone. I thought she was nervous too. I turned to the white sheet behind me for a few minutes showing the public the colored graph that appeared on it. When I turned back to the audience I looked for her once more, pointing my now expert gaze in the direction of her chair.

She was not there.

The seat was empty and she was gone.

I was out of breath. The immediate instinct to get off the stage and run out to find her was curbed by a sense of responsibility that I hated. I looked at the time, I was almost done. I could skip questions by pretending to be ill. Maybe she had gone to the bathroom and I was worried about nothing. It had to be so, why run away? She would reappear at any moment, allowing me to breathe again. Minutes passed and some people had already raised their hands waiting their turn to ask questions. Anna did not return. I looked at Paolo who gave me an investigative look, as if to ask me if I was okay. I barely smiled at him. I gave the floor to the woman in the second row who asked such an obvious question it made me think that during the course my microphone was off. I dismissed her in less than a minute. Then it was the turn of the man in the mustard-colored jacket. Another two, three minutes. The hand of the clock on the wall kept moving and the damn door wouldn't open. Anna was gone, I was sure of that. But why?

Another question and then a fourth and a fifth, the half hour was about to run out when a scruffy looking kid and a sitting in his chair in a way that bothered me asked me to explain how to make a business plan one more time. I looked at Paolo. He stood up and took the microphone saying that time was up, an e-mail with the main notions covered in the course would be sent to each of them. I thanked everyone right after him and ran out.

I checked the corridors, the rooms, the kitchen, the balcony and even the bathroom but there was no trace of Anna. I leaned against the door next to the sinks, barely holding back a scream of rage. Someone tried to open the door I was blocking, I moved to let in the man with the mustard-colored jacket.

"Congratulations, your course was amazing."

"Thanks."

"Can I ask for your e-mail to get in touch in the future?"

"No. I mean, I don't know if you are allowed to. Ask Paolo, he's the organizer."

I left the bathroom and went to the desk where I had left my backpack. I just wanted to get out of there and lock myself in my room with a case of beer.

Paolo entered the office while I was putting away the material. "It went great!" he exclaimed enthusiastically as he patted me on the shoulder.

"Yes, it went well."

"How did you feel about it?"

"As I said, it went well."

"I meant to ask if you liked it. You know... we could think about a collaboration."

"Yes, sure, why not?" I replied absently, unable to stop torturing myself for that missed opportunity.

Why had she left? What was the need? It made me angry and desperate at the same time.

A couple of Paolo's colleagues had come in to escape the crowd that had attacked the prosecco table. "Here, we stole one for you", said the tall blond guy whose name I couldn't remember, handing me the plastic stem glass.

"Cheers."

"Cheers."

"Hey, who was the woman you were talking to before the lecture?" I looked up at the guy, the same one who had given me the prosecco. *What do you care?* I wanted to answer.

"A friend."

"Not bad, your friend!" interjected the other who was short, dark and a little stocky. Standing together they looked like a comedy duo.

"Yes, she's cute."

"Cute? Come on, don't be shy, we noticed how you were looking at her."

"No... it's just that I hadn't seen her in a long time."

"Well, if I had a friend like that, I'd visit her more often."

I was bothered by the way that tall, super cool looking guy talked about Anna.

"She's married," I said resentfully.

"Yeah... well, it might be boring but it's an insignificant detail," the short guy interjected.

I got out of the conversation by turning my back to them to put the last few things in my backpack.

"In any event, she didn't have a ring on her finger so, the way I see it, no ring, no love."

I turned my head abruptly. "What did you say?"

"No ring, no..."

"No, not that, the other thing. About the ring."

"She didn't have a ring on her finger. You know, the ring on your finger, when you get married..."

"How do you know?"

"Marco has a gift," Paolo intervened. "He sees a pretty girl in the crowd and the first thing he does is check if she has a wedding ring on. He has even perfected it from a distance."

"Well… at forty it's something to check before taking the leap." A flurry of images and words invaded my brain.
Spinning her wedding ring around.
Didn't that make you want to take off your ring either?
No, it would take more.
What would it take?
Divorce.
I grabbed my backpack and ran out. Paolo had started saying something but I yelled at him that I would call him back. I had to move fast.
I reached into my pocket and pulled out her number.
Fuck, why didn't I save it on my phone?
I stopped in front of the elevator that was going up. I picked up the phone and started typing the numbers. I pushed the green button as the doors opened and went inside. The phone didn't ring, it was silent. I looked again to make sure I had started the call and saw that there was no signal. *The elevator!* I cursed.
I waited impatiently for it to get to ground floor.
It was like being locked in an hourglass with sand almost reaching your mouth, marking the end of your time.
The doors opened and I bolted out of the building.
It was ringing.
It was still ringing.
Come on, Anna, answer.
Third ring.
"Hello?"
"Why is there no wedding ring on your finger?"
"What?"
"Why don't you have a wedding ring on your finger anymore?"
"Michele."

"Yes... answer me."

Silence.

"Anna..." I took a breath and calmed down. I repeated the question in a less aggressive tone. "...just tell me why you don't have a wedding ring on your finger."

Silence.

"We broke up."

Silence.

"Where are you now?"

"I'm at the station."

"I'm coming."

Epilogue

The light of this June evening and the warm air allowed us to bring the large wooden table out into the terrace. It is set for eight, but only six people are sitting down. Adele and Pietro are playing tag, visibly happy to be together again. The string of hanging lights, hooked to the corners of the walls, forms a triangle of lights that are adding to the festive atmosphere. Although the dress was not formal, I changed to be more comfortable. From the kitchen I'm looking out at the people I most wanted by my side on this day and I feel grateful for that image. I take the pot and go out.

Lisa helps me by making room on the table where I place the paella the men have cooked. I pick up the phone and see a message from Angelo. "All my best wishes to you and Miguel". I smile and answer. "Thank you, I'm sorry you couldn't be here, we'll celebrate at the office!".

I think about how far we have come together since he suggested I manage the magazine with him. At first I was scared and I wondered if it was a risky step, but then he was able to motivate me. Seeing how much the rest of the staff, whom Angelo was able to save with that change of direction, believed in me too, had given me the courage to take the plunge. It was a blessing.

It was thanks to that new incentive that I managed to move past the separation from Lorenzo, without falling into total despair.

Back from my trip to Barcelona I had faced him asking him for the utmost sincerity and, with difficulty, I had given him mine. He had thus admitted to having suspicions about his infertility, precisely because of that unsuccessful appendicitis surgery, before which the doctor had told him about the possibility of becoming infertile. I, in turn, had been honest about the feelings I discovered I had for Miguel. We broke up after about a month.

Since then I had lived in Angelo's apartment, the one where the newsroom had been based in during the early years. I thought about Miguel every single day, looking for the strength to accept that he was another woman's fiancée. It was painful.

"To the newlyweds", Alex yells, raising his sangria glass.

"To Miguel and Anna", Federica says smiling.

Pietro runs to his mother and asks her why they can't sleep at our house.

"Because you, your dad and I are staying at a hotel", Lisa replies, caressing his face.

"But I want to stay here like Adele."

"There are more people than beds here, honey."

"Speaking of which", Alex intervenes, "...Fede, you're sleeping on the couch."

"Like hell I am... you sleep on there!"

"I have my kid with me." Alex grabs Adele as she runs beside him and cuddles her, smiling at Federica.

"I'm sleep with Auntie Fede, daddy." He looks at his daughter with a betrayed expression.

Miguel comes up behind me and holds me in his embrace, I squeeze him and bask in the moment.

"Don't worry, the couch is comfortable if you don't pay attention to its leather sticking to you."

I look at the right corner of the terrace, the painting on the easel is the presence of Miguel's mother who could not have missed this moment.

He comes closer and whispers in my ear, "Everything's perfect."

It really is.

Acknowledgements

My thanks to Giada Obelisco who was the first ever to read this novel, saving me from self-sabotage when I kept erasing line after line of a text I could no longer appreciate with clarity. Thank you, Giada, you are a professional and precise editor, you have helped me believe in a piece of work that would not have seen the light without your touch.

Thank you Domenica Lupia, an exceptional layout artist and graphic designer who, with her unlimited patience, embraced my doubts and my quirks, encouraging me not to settle even when it meant reworking everything all over again. Furthermore, thank you for your warmth and your stories of daily life that have always made me smile.

I'm grateful to Andrea Ucini, an incredible Artist and beautiful person, whom I had the pleasure of meeting in his gallery and who I have not stopped following since that day. I am honored and grateful that you designed the cover of my book.

My thanks to this magnificent city, Copenhagen, for encouraging me to make my dream come true: its places, its magic and its peacefulness made me believe that it was possible.

In my private life I would like to thank with all my heart the people who have followed with enthusiasm and sincere interest every progress of this undertaking: my friends. It is true that, living away from home, the friends we meet become like family and that is what you are for me. Thank you Claire, Nicolaj, Maite, Jordi, Rob and Natalie.

Elisa and Serena who, just like sisters, have been with me for a lifetime and whom I could not imagine my life without. Thank you for your encouragement, for your valuable revisions to the text and above all thank you for always being there for me.

Valentina, always ready to go into battle to protect the ones she loves. Thanks for inspiring the character that bears your name.

My family, of origin and extended, which although far away is still the most beautiful place to come back to.

To Filippo and Cloe, who have always been my source of inspiration, as well as infinite joy. Thank you, Filippo, for often asking me how my book was coming along, and thank you, Cloe, for saying you want to learn to read in order to read it.

I am grateful to Tomaso, a husband who gently tried to enter a project I have kept secret for a long time, perhaps for too long. Thank you for being able to wait, for listening to me even though I didn't know what I was talking about and thank you for the enthusiasm you showed when I finally asked you to read my book. Thank you for also giving me the time and space to make it happen.

Thank you, reader, for doing me the honor of holding this book in your hands.